THE DISTILLER'S DARLING

THE RIVER HILL SERIES

REBECCA NORINNE

JAMAILA BRINKLEY

ABOUT THIS BOOK

Welcome back to River Hill, where love comes when you least expect it.

River Hill is an unlikely place to launch a whiskey empire, but Irishman Iain Brennan's just reckless enough to make it work. And finding out the dark-haired artist he spent one glorious night with lives across town is an added bonus. Since he's never said no to mixing business with pleasure, hiring her to design his labels is the best decision he's made in ages—especially since she's even less interested in a relationship than he is.

Naomi Klein may have put down roots in River Hill, but she's not looking for happily-ever-after. Just the idea of forever gives her hives. Which makes a rootless Irish wanderer in town for three months the perfect fling. The fact that he's happy to let her focus on her art makes spending time with him even more appealing. And shocking her society mother? Just a bonus.

But as cozy autumn nights turn into lazy winter mornings, Iain and Naomi realize they've done the unthinkable and fallen in love! Neither are ready to settle down, but settling for a life without the other is out of the question. Or is it?

CONTENTS

1

"*W*ell, *that* just happened." Naomi Klein sipped her champagne as she watched her date practically vault across the dance floor in pursuit of another woman. She smiled fondly.

Noah Bradstone was one of her best friends, and she had reason to know he was damned good in bed, but he was going to have to be a hell of a lot more than a nice dick in a tailored suit if he wanted to land Angelica Travis. The former actress was building a hotel next door to Noah's vineyard, and he'd fallen head over heels for her the second she yelled at him. *A man with mommy issues,* Naomi reflected with a grin.

"I'm not sure I believe what I just heard," came a female voice from next to her.

Speak of the devil.

Naomi turned to find Noah's mother, Bernice Winchester Bradstone. Bernice was also Naomi's mother's best friend; sleeping with Noah had always felt the tiniest bit incestuous—not that he'd noticed or cared.

The man's ability to ignore the things other people stressed about was something Naomi found equally exasperating and endearing. It was one reason she hadn't put an end to their extracurriculars years before.

She'd been perfectly happy with their now-and-then friends-with-benefits situation, but she'd long suspected Noah needed more. Just not from her. Much as he pretended to be a footloose and fancy-free commitment-phobe, Noah wanted long-term … whether he knew it or not. He was chasing picket fences, and Naomi sincerely hoped Angelica would be the one to give them to him.

She, however, wanted nothing to do with any of that. Just thinking about being with one person for the rest of her life—or even the rest of the year—gave her hives.

"Not what you expected?" she asked Bernice.

The older woman pursed her lips, colored to perfection with Chanel's quintessential red. "Not at all."

"Disappointed?"

"Not exactly. It's always a surprise when your children find happiness in a way you don't expect. When you're the one who raised them, you think you know them." Her expression turned thoughtful. "But you want them to be happy, however they get there." She smiled, and patted Naomi's shoulder fondly. "You'll know what I mean someday."

Not likely.

Naomi kept a smile pasted on her face and nodded vaguely. She had no interest in children whatsoever, and it wasn't because she just hadn't met The One, as her mother frequently asserted.

"I see my parents," she told Bernice, effectively cutting

that line of conversation off at the pass. "Talk to you soon." She exchanged the customary cheek kiss and made her way across the room to find her parents, her brother, and his wife standing in a cluster near the finger food.

The Doctors Klein made an imposing pair. Her father was the head of cardiology at San Francisco General, and her brother looked like a younger, slightly more muscular clone. Both had thick, dark hair that lay in gentle waves tamed by expensive cuts, and each had a beautiful woman on his arm.

"Hey, Nay," her brother said. "Single again?"

She resisted the urge to flip him the bird. The only deviation Jacob had ever made from The Klein Plan was to marry Tanya Deuterhorn instead of the Nice Jewish Girl their parents had picked out for him, and since Tanya had immediately converted and was currently making raising their three children look easy *and* keeping the books part-time for Jacob's celebrity-studded plastic surgery practice, he'd been swiftly forgiven.

Naomi, on the other hand, had been deviating from The Plan since she was five years old, when she'd demanded to go to art camp instead of ballet class.

"I was already single," she answered.

"Please, don't remind me." Her mother raised the back of her wrist to her forehead in a sign of mock distress. "What happened over there?"

Judith Klein was the perfect doctor's wife and the ultimate socialite. She and Bernice ran their inner circle with gilded fists, and the Founders' Ball was their cornerstone event. Naomi was well aware that the prodigal daughter's date fleeing her side was not a good look for the family. While Naomi didn't particularly care about the impression she gave, Noah didn't deserve her mother's censure.

"I think Noah's in love," she said with a grin.

"He ought to be in love with *you*," her mother answered stiffly. Their two mothers had been planning their wedding since Naomi and Noah had gotten stuck in an elevator together at her bat mitzvah.

"Please," Jacob said with a mock shudder. "Noah's a great guy, but there's literally nobody I want less as a brother-in-law."

"That's just because you don't like wine," his wife said. "That Prodigy Pinot he made a few years ago was incredible." Tanya was a fan of Stonewell Vineyards, Noah's winery, and was a loyal customer, something that made Naomi love her almost as much as the fact that she never tried to set her up on blind dates.

"Give me hard liquor anytime," Jacob said, raising the small, tulip-shaped glass in his hand to catch the light. "Have you tried this one, Dad?"

Their father nodded. "It's straight from Ireland. Your mother heard about it from one of her cronies." He gave his wife a fond smile to take the sting out of his words. "The only thing I ask in return for my presence at these things is good whiskey."

Naomi resisted the urge to snort. As though he wouldn't have been here anyway. He was gunning hard for the Chief of Staff position at the hospital, and every single member of the Board of Directors attended the Founders' Ball. There was a very good reason her mother

co-chaired the gala committee. The Klein Plan, in full
effect.

"I wouldn't mind buying some of it," Jacob said idly,
swirling his glass again and lifting it to his nose.

"I'll get you the information, but I don't think it's
available here yet," his mother replied impatiently. "Can
we get back to the real issue here?"

"What issue?"

"Your sister."

"I'm an issue? Gee, thanks, Mom," Naomi said.

"Darling girl, you've been an issue all your life and
you're proud of it," her mother said, fondness mixing with
exasperation in her voice. "Noah Bradstone aside, are you
ever going to settle down?"

"I'm totally settled!" Naomi protested. "I have a
mortgage!" She'd bought a cute craftsman bungalow in
River Hill a few years ago, having decided she needed a
home base instead of constantly traveling back and forth
between studio and gallery residencies. She still spent a
lot of time away from home, but at least she had one.
Every time she pulled into the driveway, she felt like an
honest-to-goodness grownup. And the studio space she'd
converted the attic into was gorgeous. Her art had
definitely improved since then, and the galleries she
routinely worked with seemed to agree—she'd already
had to fend off one owner tonight. He was set on buying a
sculpture she'd intended to auction off, but his offer
hadn't been good enough to keep her from moving on to
the hors d'oeuvres table.

Her mother sniffed. "A tiny house in that ridiculous
tourist town."

"River Hill isn't a tourist town. It's just not San Francisco."

"Mom can't imagine anybody not wanting to live here," Jacob said, gesturing wide to indicate all the glitz and glamour surrounding them. "If you leave the city, you might see the outdoors and breathe air that doesn't smell like cars and piss. Can't have that."

His wife elbowed him. "Hush."

"If you'd ever actually *visit* River Hill, you'd like it, Mom," Naomi said. "Jacob and Tanya have been."

"There's a really good restaurant there," Tanya said supportively. "Right in the town square."

Her mother shuddered theatrically. "Any town small enough to have a square is too small for me."

It would certainly be too small for the both of them, Naomi thought. Heck, the seven square miles that made up *San Francisco* had been too small, which was one of the many reasons she'd made her home a couple of hours away in the first place. It was the exact right distance to keep her family at bay.

"And if you're not going to marry Noah, how are you going to meet somebody all the way out there?" Her mother was still talking, unfortunately.

"Can we not argue about me meeting somebody in the middle of the Founders' Ball, please?"

"Why not? I thought it was an annual tradition." Her brother grinned.

"Shut up, Jacob," Naomi and her mother snapped in unison.

"Ah, there's the other annual tradition," her father said, and Tanya giggled.

"I hear you like our whiskey," a new voice interjected. Deep and smooth, it sounded rather like Jacob always said whiskey tasted.

Naomi turned, and found her mouth suddenly dry. The most delicious man she'd ever seen was standing next to her, holding three glasses of whiskey in one huge hand. He was nearly the same height she was in her black, strappy, four-inch heels, which made him shorter than her father and brother. Solidly built, he filled out his tux to perfection. Some attempt had been made to tame the brown beard that rose above the snowy white points of his shirt, but nothing could disguise the laugh lines carved deep around his eyes. A few freckles were visible beneath his light tan, and his hair had been artfully mussed. The muscles in his broad shoulders shifted, and she glanced down at the drinks he was offering them. Somehow, his palm managed to cradle the bases of all three glasses while his fingers balanced between their edges, holding them safely. She stared blankly at his hand, feeling a tiny zinging sensation down her spine that led straight to curiosity: what would those hands feel like on *her*?

Naomi managed to drag her eyes back up to his face, which didn't help much, because his warm blue eyes were on her, too. She wondered if he was thinking the same wickedly delicious thoughts.

"I don't like whiskey," she blurted, and his eyes crinkled in an easy smile.

Passing two glasses to her father and brother, the man held onto the third. "Is that so?"

She shrugged, attempting to recapture her usual cool. "Sorry, never have."

"It would be an acquired taste," he said, raising the glass to his nose with an easy swirl before inhaling. "But I came out of the womb reaching for a dram." His Irish accent was obvious now, and she found herself wanting to hear him talk more.

Jacob snorted. "An acquired taste. Sounds like you, sis."

"Are you done?" she snapped, feeling heat rising in her cheeks—and elsewhere.

Her silk dress—which put the 'little' in little black dress—didn't leave much to the imagination, and if she didn't quickly bring her body's reactions under control, the sexy stranger trying to ply her with booze was going to know *exactly* how she responded to him. She could feel her nipples turning into hard little points beneath the thin fabric.

Although maybe that wasn't such a bad thing, she thought, letting her gaze roam over him again as he exchanged pleasantries with her family. It had been a while since she'd come across someone who made her heart beat like a herd of wild horses running at full gallop, and this man—with his rugged good looks and Irish accent that was out of place in this posh San Francisco ballroom—certainly qualified in that regard.

Naomi didn't spend a lot of time in society, but when she did, she felt nearly as much of a stranger as he seemed to be. She'd escaped her parents' inner circle a long time ago, and these days she was accustomed to a much more private way of life. One that didn't mean she had to pretend to be meek and demure and wait for men to get around to thinking about *her* wants and desires. She had an active sex drive, and she used it well and often, something her mother would probably be horrified to know. As far as Naomi was concerned, as long as everybody involved was a consenting adult and nobody was married, she was more than happy with the way things were.

She might be even happier if she could convince the sexy Irishman to join her for a nightcap. Provided, of course, it wasn't whiskey.

2

*I*ain surveyed the sexy American with renewed interest. He'd been eyeing her all evening. Hearing her give as good as she got had him itching to know more about her. The woman had fire. And he liked it.

"At the risk of sounding like a cliche," Iain whispered, shifting closer to her side while her brother laughed about a joke he'd just told at her expense, "can I get you a drink —one that's not my family's whiskey?"

She glanced at her parents, who were in deep conversation with the other couple, and shrugged. "Sure, that'd be great." Without saying goodbye, she turned and walked away, clearly expecting Iain to follow.

Which he was more than happy to do. She was stunning from the front, but the back of her dress—a network of criss-crossed silver beaded strands that shimmered with each step she took—was a work of art that rippled over her flesh, hugging her in all the right places.

Iain lengthened his stride to catch up and held out his hand. "I'm Iain, by the way. I'm afraid I didn't catch your name back there."

Moving into a corner where they were partially hidden from the crowd by a potted palm, she stuck out her hand in return. "Naomi. And it's nice to meet you."

Iain took Naomi's hand in his, and was unnerved to feel an instant, white-hot bolt of … something … travel straight to his gut. He didn't believe in love at first sight, but there was definitely *something* between them. Some unexplainable chemistry he'd never felt with anyone before—and he was desperate to explore it further.

Preferably somewhere her family *wasn't* nearby, and a bed *was*.

"About that drink I promised—"

"—What do you say we get out of here, and go somewhere less stuffy?" she interrupted before he could suggest the very same thing.

They smiled at one another, and then Naomi looked away briefly before setting her fingers to her mouth. Dropping her hand, she said, "I'm sorry. That probably sounded awfully forward." She didn't sound particularly sorry, though, Iain noted.

"Not at all." He grinned. "In fact, I was just about to ask if you wanted to get out of here. I know this little bar down the street that makes the best cocktails—"

"Gibson's?" she asked, her eyes catching the light and twinkling like the crystal in the chandeliers above.

"Yeah, you know it?"

"Oh, Iain," she laughed, setting her hand to his arm.

"Everyone knows Gibson's. It's the hottest place in town right now."

"Oh." He should have known she would already know all the best places in San Francisco. That he'd honestly thought he'd stumbled on an undiscovered gem after spending thirty minutes with the barman earlier that afternoon made him feel a bit foolish. He should have known better. After all, he'd practically *been* that barman once.

She stepped out of their alcove and tossed him a smile over her shoulder. "Come on, let's grab my wrap and we can head out. If you like Gibson's, I'll show you somewhere even better."

Thirty minutes later, they were tucked into a dark booth in the back of a bar Iain wasn't sure should still be standing. The floor was slanted, the walls were bowed, and the patchy ceiling wasn't much taller than the woman sitting next to him. He'd been in some questionable establishments over the years—including a pub built into a cave where monks used to hide out from raiding hordes—but this one took the prize for 'most likely to crumble in on itself.'

Looking around, he blew out a whistle. "This is …"

"A death trap?" She laughed again, a warm sound he was growing to enjoy.

Once they'd left the ball, Naomi's whole demeanor had changed. Her shoulders had instantly relaxed, and her eyes looked less wary, like she wasn't constantly on guard. She hadn't said anything, but he got the sense she didn't enjoy those fancy events nearly as much as her family wished she might. Honestly, he could relate.

"That's exactly what I was going to say."

"Yeah, I'm pretty sure if there's a bad earthquake, we're dead." She looked around the joint, her face happy and her eyes bright. "Although, come to think of it, this building's been here since before 1906, so we're probably safe."

"1906? Oh, the earthquake?" Upon touching down in San Francisco last week, Iain had quickly learned there were three topics of conversation you could safely embark on if you found yourself in conversation with a stranger here: the weather (it was great), technology (it was either life-changing or the root of all evil, depending on your audience), and when "the big one" might hit. Apparently, there'd been something everyone called "a four-point-two" the day before he'd landed, causing some damage in Berkeley, and it had people on edge.

"One and the same," she said, tossing back the last of her gin and tonic. Iain didn't like to brag, but he thought the gin his family made was slightly more flavorful. Then again, he supposed he wasn't at all impartial.

"I can't imagine living like that, always on the verge of disaster without any warning."

"Oh, it's not too bad. The worst we've had since 1989 is a little bit of the bed rocking in the middle of the night." There was a beat of silence, then Naomi's eyes went wide with recognition at what she'd just said. She laughed again. "Oh, no, you probably think …"

Iain eyed her over the rim of his glass. "That you have a fantastic sense of humor and are utterly delightful. Not to mention incredibly beautiful."

She eyed him back, her expression quickly shifting from jovial to thoughtful. "I'm just going to put this out there—and you can tell me I'm insane for even suggesting it—but do you want to go back to my hotel?"

Iain tried to play it cool, but he was definitely surprised. He'd been hoping that's how the night would end, but he'd assumed he'd be the one to make a move … a few hours from now. From the time they'd walked through the door of the pub, he'd known he was going to fuck Naomi, he just hadn't known *when*. He was confident in who he was. He was never going to be the best-looking lad in the room, but he had something no other man here did: an Irish accent. Personally, he didn't see what the big deal was, but across several continents, it was a sure-fire panty-dropper.

He set his glass to the side and captured her gaze. "Just so I'm clear here, you're asking me back to your room so we can make the bed do a little rocking in the middle of the night?" His lips hitched to the side in a smirk, while hers did the same. He appreciated that she appreciated his bad joke.

"Yes, exactly. I'd also like to make the walls rattle a bit, if you're up for it."

"You really are the most delightful woman I've ever met," he said, sliding out of the booth and tossing a handful of bills on the sticky table before reaching out and taking her hand. "I promise to do my best to bring security down on our heads."

As they stumbled out onto the sidewalk, a dense fog snaked its way around them, wrapping their bodies in a misty cold. Naomi shivered, and pulled her flimsy black wrap tighter around her bare arms. Iain stepped behind her and circled her middle with his arms. With her hair up in an intricate knot, he had perfect access to her neck.

"I've been wanting to taste you all night," he said, dropping a soft, open-mouthed kiss to the skin just below her ear. "And here," he added, dotting kisses up the length of her long, delicate neck.

She shivered once more, and this time not from the cold. "Do that again."

His tongue flicked out and licked a path from her spine to her nape. "If you taste this sweet here," he said, trailing his lips along her shoulder, "I can't wait to taste you here." His hand skated its way down, down, down.

"Oh God, that's hot." She melted into his embrace. "Where's that damn Uber?"

"Where's your hotel?"

She jutted out her chin. "Down the hill, in SoMA."

Damn. They definitely needed a cab. There was no way Naomi was walking that far in those spikes she called shoes. Reluctantly dragging his lips from her heated skin, Iain scanned their surroundings. He couldn't be sure, but he *thought* they might not be too far from where he was staying.

"Is this Nob Hill?"

She chuckled. "Sure. Or the Tender-Nob. Or the Nobber-Loin. Take your pick."

"How far is Union Square?"

"A couple of blocks. Why?"

He pulled her in tight against him. Tight enough, he knew, that she'd be able to feel his erection straining against his trousers. He wanted this woman, and she wanted him. And neither of them wanted to wait. "I'm staying at the Westin. We could—"

Before he had time to explain his line of thinking, Naomi had stepped out of his hold, grabbed his hand, and was marching them quickly down the street. He'd never seen a woman move so quickly and so effortlessly in shoes like that, but he wasn't about to complain. Clearly, she wanted this as much as he did.

"I—"

"Shh, no talking." She shot him an apologetic smile. "Sorry, that was rude. I'm just super keyed up right now and I don't want to lose that feeling. We'll be in your hotel room in approximately ten minutes, and hopefully you'll be inside of me a few minutes after that. I don't want to make it awkward with small talk."

Christ. What was that he'd thought earlier about love at first sight? Because the more he got to know Naomi, the more he liked about her. Actually, honestly liked. When you factored in her no-bullshit stance toward sex, he thought he might even be half in love with her. All in the course of one evening. Provided that sort of thing actually happened in real life. But since it didn't, he pulled her hand to his lips and kissed her palm, his tongue flicking out at the last second to give her a brief preview of what she could expect in approximately thirteen minutes.

Because while he couldn't wait to sink his cock inside of her, he didn't want to rush things either. He'd told her he wanted to taste her, and he hadn't been lying. Iain had a very refined palate, and he planned to spend several long moments identifying all the unique flavors that comprised Miss Naomi.

When she moaned and squeezed his hand in a vice grip before increasing their pace, Iain chuckled to himself. *Yeah, we're on the exact same page.*

Six minutes later (but who was counting?) they sailed through the doors of the hotel and into the grand lobby. Without breaking stride, Naomi made her way straight to the elevator bay, and pressed the button.

"You come here often?" Iain felt an unexpected bolt of jealousy. He knew this was a one-night stand and that they were both sexual beings, but he didn't like the reminder of just *how* sexual Naomi might actually be. That probably made him a chauvinist pig, but he didn't think she'd want to be confronted with the evidence of his past partners either.

Her eyes found his, and immediately the heat in them cooled. "Yes, many times. Is that a problem?"

He didn't like the implication of that frosty statement, but he liked the idea of them parting ways even less. He didn't want to say goodbye without learning just how hot their fire burned. If it was even half as potent as he thought it might be, their night together would be worth it. And besides, it wasn't like he was going to marry this girl; what, and who, they'd done before they'd met had no bearing on the things they were about to do to one another in the here and now. All he needed to do now was wrap it up and enjoy the ride.

"No problem at all," he said as the door chimed and then slid open. Placing his hand on the small of her back, over where her dress dipped deliciously low in the back, he guided her inside the compartment.

When the doors shut, he pressed the button for his floor and she turned to him. "I don't come here to—"

He stepped into her space, backing her up against the wall. "It doesn't matter," he growled, nipping at her lush bottom lip and tugging it between his teeth. "I want you, and I intend to have you. I don't care about anything else."

Naomi's head fell back with a moan, and she speared her fingers through his hair, holding him close while he feasted on her skin. With his attention focused on her dainty collar bone, Iain slid the strap of her dress down her shoulder where it pooled at her elbow. The fabric slipped down her skin with a slight *whoosh*, exposing her nipple to his hungry mouth. When he sucked it between his lips, she mewled, the sound going straight to his dick.

"Has anyone ever told you that you have an exceptionally talented mouth?" she asked, her words coming out in between pants and moans.

He flicked the pert, dusky pink nub with his tongue and winked. "You ain't seen nothing yet."

3

Naomi opened one eye and examined the ceiling until she remembered where she was. *Ah, yes. The gala. The hotel. The Irishman. Yum.* She yawned and stretched, feeling the burn of muscles well-used. Iain's elevator antics had been just the start of their fun last night.

Fortunately, his room was only on the fifth floor. The elevator's security cameras might have burst into flames if they'd traveled any higher. They'd stumbled out of the compartment and down the hall in a haze of lust, and her dress and his pants had dropped on top of each other right inside the door to his room. And then … *well.*

Naomi pointed her toes and smiled, feeling satisfaction spread like warmth through her body as the muscles in her legs stretched and loosened.

Iain had made good on his dirty promises of a feast. Her body had been appetizer, entrée, and dessert, and then she'd happily returned the favor. They'd spent a great deal of time gasping, panting for breath, and moaning—and quite a bit of time laughing as well.

On the whole, definitely a night to remember.

And now it was time for the part that sometimes turned awkward: leaving.

She turned in the bed, and found Iain watching her through lowered lashes. "Hello."

"Good morning." He reached out a lazy arm and wrapped it around her waist, tugging her body flush against his.

She relaxed against his warmth for a moment, then stretched up for a quick kiss. "Can I use your shower?"

"Be my guest," he said with a yawn.

She slid out of the bed with a final pat on his extremely well-muscled thigh. "Thanks."

Knowing Iain was watching her walk naked through the room, she put a bit of flair into her bend as she snagged her dress from the floor on the way into the bathroom. She heard a quick intake of breath behind her and grinned. It was nice to leave a lasting impression.

She closed the door behind her and flipped on the shower spray, letting the water warm up before she stepped in. She took advantage of the tiny hotel-branded shampoo and conditioner bottles set decoratively in the soap dish; Iain either wasn't the sort of man to use anything but his own hair products, or he hadn't been here long enough to need them yet. She was betting on both, actually. She worked the conditioner into her hair, grimacing at the familiar scent.

Her parents' penthouse was near here, so she frequently stayed at this hotel when she came to the city to visit. She certainly wasn't staying with them. Letting her mother have the opportunity to eavesdrop on her comings and goings was something she'd learned to avoid years ago. So she stayed in a hotel, or once in a great while in Jacob and Tanya's guest room if she thought she was up to being pummeled by several sets of tiny fists at six o'clock in the morning.

But her parents would probably be selling their place soon, she reflected. Her mother's favorite hobby—aside from interfering in her children's lives and supporting her husband's ambitions, of course—was buying properties and re-decorating them. Naomi had to admit that her mom had impeccable taste. Judith Klein would probably be horrified to hear it, but Naomi was pretty sure that her artistic talent had come from her mother. *Naomi, my dear, art is very well for a hobby. But you need to have goals.* Her mother's voice echoed in her head.

Naomi finished rinsing the conditioner out of her hair and smirked. Turns out, she did have goals. She'd met a lot of them, in fact, and then dreamed up more. And the gallery owner she was meeting in a few hours was the key to her next one. She'd picked her hotel for this trip to be closer to that meeting than the gala and her parents, but she'd wound up here anyway. Funny how things worked out. She hardly minded, though. A shower here, and a stop at her hotel to change clothes and check out, and she'd be on her way to being the next featured artist at Z Gallery.

She soaped and rinsed her body quickly, smiling as her fingers met the flesh Iain's clever hands had shaped the night before. As a sculptor, Naomi knew all about how to mold a person's curves, and Iain was damn talented at it. She shut the water off, then squeezed the dripping length of her hair over the drain until it seemed safe to step out of the tub without creating a flood. She reached past the curtain toward where the towels were folded, but when her hand encountered flesh instead of terrycloth, she yelped in surprise.

"Not every morning a man gets goosed when he goes to piss," Iain's voice came from beyond the shower curtain. He sounded amused.

"Sorry! Can you hand me a towel?"

"Here." His hand came through the curtain holding the white towel, still folded. "Sure you don't want me to return the favor?"

She took the towel and laughed as she wrapped it around her body. "You're too kind." She swept the curtain open. "Hand me another?"

"Here you are."

She took the second towel and bent to wrap it around her hair, twisting it quickly before she straightened. "Thanks." She stepped out of the tub, giving in to her baser impulses and fastening her hands on his hips to balance herself.

He reached back and palmed her breast through the towel. "Still nice," he murmured. He turned to face her fully, and she saw that he was hard again. "One more for the road?"

She was tempted, but she had a schedule to keep. She reached down and stroked him twice. "I can't."

He lowered his head to rest his forehead against hers. "Cruel woman."

"Successful woman." She reached further and tickled the sensitive area behind his balls, and he hissed in a breath.

"I stand by my previous statement." He grabbed her hand and ignored her grin. "If you're not going to do anything with that, put it away. You can't go waving deadly weapons around like that."

She laughed. "Sorry. I have a meeting."

He looked her up and down, towel and all. "What kind of meeting?"

"What, you don't conduct business in the nude?"

"Depends on the business." He pinched her bottom as she turned to leave the bathroom. "Want to buy some whiskey?"

"Not today." Her dress muffled her voice as she tugged it over her head. "I think I've had plenty of Irish in me for the day."

"You can never have enough Irish in you." He followed her out of the bathroom and gave a tug to the hem of her dress. "There you go. That's straight."

"Thank you."

"My pleasure. You need anything?"

"My wrap?"

"On the chair." His voice was muffled now as he shrugged into a t-shirt he'd pulled from the carry-on suitcase lying open on the luggage stand. She hadn't noticed it last night, since her eyes had been focused on the man who owned it.

"Not staying long?" She didn't see any other bags.

"Flying out this afternoon, actually. Got meetings up in Seattle."

She didn't press. His business, whatever it was, wasn't hers, and she didn't know anybody in Washington other than a few artists who lived in a commune outside Walla-Walla. She didn't think they wanted any whiskey, though. They had a well-known preference for mushrooms as their artistic muse.

"Have a good trip," she said.

"Have a good meeting," he answered.

"I intend to."

She didn't offer him her number, or her card, and he didn't seem inclined to give her his, either. What luck! A one-night stand who was literally only in town for one night? She definitely wouldn't be running into him again. And while she might have enjoyed a repeat of last night—who was she kidding, she would *love* a repeat of last night—she was far more interested in avoiding awkward prolonged goodbyes, painful hints about what she was doing next weekend, or a never-ending series of text messages.

Naomi beamed at Iain. He was the perfect man. Sexy, great with his hands, and gone the next day. She gathered her things while he finished dressing, and then gave him a quick kiss. "Thanks for a great night, Iain."

"Thank *you*," he said. "I appreciate the introduction to San Francisco."

She laughed. "Nobody better to make you feel at home than a native."

"I'll return the favor next time you're in Ireland."

"You've got it." She chuckled, knowing neither of them meant it.

"Shall I see you out?"

She shook her head. "No, thanks. I've got it." She pulled out her phone and checked the time. "Gotta get moving, though." By some miracle her mother had only texted her once overnight. She ignored it, like she usually did. Communication with her mother required coffee. "Safe travels."

"You too," he said, opening the door for her. As she passed him, she felt his hand close around the left side of her butt and squeeze firmly. "Just a little reminder."

She laughed and extracted herself from his grip. "I'll remember."

"Oh, that was for me."

The last thing she saw before he closed the door were the crinkles around his eyes and mouth as he grinned at her.

---

*E*ight o'clock in the morning in the Westin lobby was a far different place to be wearing her tiny, sexy gala dress than last night had been. Naomi hated the phrase 'walk of shame,' since she tried never to do anything she was ashamed of. But stalking through the ornate marble lobby in her sky-high heels without the benefit of caffeine was really asking too much. She found the complimentary coffee bar outside the breakfast area and poured herself a cup while she tapped out her Uber request for a ride to her hotel. She made a face after the first sip. Hopefully it would be the only bad part of her day.

"That's no way to look at a perfectly innocent cup of

coffee." The voice was familiar, and unfortunate. The coffee wasn't nearly good enough to be worth tolerating her brother this early in the day.

She'd almost forgotten that Jacob and Tanya were staying here for the gala weekend, to be closer to the event and have a kid-free weekend. It was the other reason she'd decided *not* to stay at this hotel.

"Can't be that innocent. She isn't a hotel guest, remember?" Her sister-in-law, as usual, dove right in.

Naomi sighed and turned. "Hi. You have three minutes to make as many jokes as you can." She held up her phone to show them the blue progress line that indicated her driver was nearly there. "Not you, Jacob, I know you can't perform well under pressure." She aimed her fakest, kindly-caring-sister smile at him.

"Ouch," he protested. "That was uncalled for."

"I've had literally one sip of terrible coffee."

"And you've been up all night?" Tanya grinned at her.

"I used to think you were so nice," Naomi told her mournfully. "I think my brother has corrupted you."

"Other way around," Jacob said. "But if you want to talk about corruption—"

"Too late. Uber's here." Naomi grinned. "Catch you later. Got a gallery to sell to." She escaped before they could figure out how to make that into a euphemism at her expense and fled through the hotel doors to her waiting ride.

Four hours later, she sat in her own car and smiled gleefully at the contract in her hand and the check clipped to the front of it. Maybe she should start drinking whiskey. Or have sex with more Irishmen. Or something.

Because that had been the most successful sale she'd ever made. The gallery had contracted her for nearly everything currently in her studio, as well as three exclusive pieces. She was going to be *busy* for the next few months. She couldn't wait to get home and start working.

4

───────

*** Three months later ***

With a sigh, Iain hefted his tired body onto a stool and then rested his elbows on the gleaming copper bar top. During his brief trip home for Christmas, his father had told him he had three months left to prove that his plan for an experimental second label of the family's whiskey was a sound financial move. But between the jet lag and near-constant headache he'd experienced since leaving his brother's place in Wicklow, he needed to spend at least a few of those ninety days getting back to his old self. Until he did, he wouldn't be much good at his job anyhow.

He'd chosen River Hill as his new base of operations after reading an article in the airline's in-flight magazine about Angelica Travis, an actress he'd seen in a few movies years ago, renovating an old estate into a high-end bed and breakfast. The reporter who'd written the piece couldn't say enough good things about the inn, its owner, or the town. An hour and a half outside of San Francisco, the Oakwell Inn was the perfect place to recharge his batteries. Thankfully, with it being low season and mid-week, they'd had a room available.

The first thing he'd done after setting his suitcase down was head to Frankie's, a restaurant famed for making the best carnitas around. According to the article, its owner, Max Vergaras, was one of the hottest up-and-coming chefs in the state. The article had also mentioned something about how he was mixing artisanal alcohol with fresh, local, seasonal ingredients to create a truly innovative cocktail menu. Iain might be famished, but he still knew how to do his job. A visit to Frankie's was good for his belly and for business.

"What can I get you?" the dark-haired man behind the bar asked, passing him a glass of ice water. Once of the things Iain loved most about visiting America was that practically every restaurant served their water ice cold. There were few things worse than drinking room temperature water.

"According to an article I just read on the plane out here, the only answer to that question is the carnitas tacos."

The man's lips hitched to the side. "Ah. That'd be the one about Angelica's place."

Iain nodded. "I'm staying there for a handful of days before heading down to San Francisco for business."

"Good choice." The other man pushed his hand forward. "I'm Max, by the way. I own this joint."

Iain leaned forward and extended his palm. "Iain Brennan. Nice place you've got here." With exposed brick walls, rough-hewn beams, and lots of copper fixtures on display, Frankie's was a perfect blend of rustic and industrial. He'd always thought if he ever opened his own distillery one day, he'd want it to look just like this.

"Thanks." Max smiled and pulled his hand back across the bar. "And here comes Angelica's boyfriend, Noah Bradstone. Feel free to tell him to fuck off when he grumbles about you being in his seat." The smirk he flashed let Iain know he was kidding, but it didn't quite prepare him for the other man's gruff greeting.

Noah reached over the bar, grabbed a bottle and a shot glass, and then dropped onto a stool next to him. "She's killing me, man."

"What happened now?" Max asked, visibly fighting a smile.

Amused, Iain watched as Noah, a big man with wide shoulders and strong, work-roughened hands, let out a frustrated groan and poured himself two fingers' worth of the amber liquid. "I told her when she gets back next week, we should quit dicking around and just go get married already."

"How romantic. I can't imagine why she's not rushing back."

Noah waved Max's sarcastic remark aside. "She said, 'Sure, that sounds great,' and then went back to talking about the show. How did I manage to find the one woman in all of California who's even less interested in getting married than I am?"

Max looked at his friend with a raised eyebrow. "You think she doesn't want to marry you? I don't know, Noah

… Angelica loves you. You guys are sickening when you're together."

"Don't get me wrong. Angelica loves me; that's not the problem. She couldn't care less about a wedding, though."

Iain fought a smile as he dug into his tacos. Frankly, he could appreciate a woman like Angelica Travis. Unbidden, his mind flashed to the Founders' Ball in San Francisco three months earlier. Sex with Naomi had been among the very best Iain had ever had, but the absolute *best* part was that she hadn't asked for his phone number or made a big deal about seeing him again. Hell, Naomi's forthright manner had been half the reason things had been so explosive between them. She'd known exactly what she wanted—and what she didn't— and hadn't been afraid to tell him. Their goodbye the next morning had been easy and uncomplicated, and he'd walked out of the hotel whistling, knowing he'd always remember the stunning brunette with great fondness. Now that he was heading back to the city, he wondered what the chances were of running into her again. Not that he'd go looking, but if their paths should cross, he wouldn't turn down a few more naked hours with her.

"So, are you two getting married next week, or not?" Max asked, calling Iain's attention back to the conversation taking place between the other two men. The one he only felt mildly guilty for eavesdropping on.

Noah grunted. "Fuck if I know. Maybe? You should probably get your good suit dry-cleaned just in case." He threw back his double shot and winced as the liquid burned a path to his belly. Slamming the glass down onto the bar, he grimaced. "That stuff's shit. Why do you serve it?"

Max reached across the bar and grabbed the unlabeled bottle, stashing it under the counter in one smooth movement. "We don't. It was a sample the guys from Bottleworks dropped off for me to try."

Noah scrubbed his palm over his mouth as if to wipe away the bad taste. "I get what they're doing and why, but just because you *want* to make hooch doesn't mean you should. You can't just throw a bunch of crap together and assume it's going to work."

Iain laughed at Noah's observation, which had the other man swiveling around to face him. Iain hadn't noticed it at first, but up close, he couldn't shake the feeling they'd met somewhere before. That didn't make any sense, though. This was his first time in River Hill. Still, there was definitely something familiar about the man, and it wasn't just his opinion about alcohol. "If everyone thought like you, my job would be so much easier."

"How so?"

"My family's in the whiskey business."

"Oh yeah? Anything I'd know?"

Iain laughed and, like he'd done with Max a few minutes before, extended his hand. "Iain Brennan."

Noah's eyebrows shot up. "No shit," he said, dwarfing Iain's palm in his. "The first time I ever drank whiskey, your name was on the bottle."

"I hear that a lot." Iain grinned, letting the faint, familiar discomfort wash through him and disappear.

He wasn't ashamed of his family name but he didn't

like using it to open doors for him, either. There was a market for a more approachable style that would entice non-whiskey drinkers, and he wanted to launch it without relying on the Brennan name. Unfortunately, his dad and brothers hadn't come around to his way of thinking. Iain was doing everything in his power to convince his family to give the new expression his brilliant sister had developed an opportunity to stand on its own merits—devoid of the proud, historic Brennan name.

"Is that the business that brings you out this way?" Max asked, setting out a bottle of wine and uncorking it.

Iain nodded. "Yeah, I'm trying to launch a new label." He exhaled. "It's a bit more complicated than that, actually, but I'm out here in an effort to convince my dad and brothers there's a market for it."

"Sounds familiar," Noah said, his face turning thoughtful.

"How so?" Iain's eyes swiveled between Max and Noah.

Instead of answering, however, Noah reached across the bar, this time taking hold of the wine Max had uncorked. Grabbing two glasses, he poured some of the ruby liquid into one, and then the other before passing it to Iain. "This is mine."

Iain wasn't a big wine drinker, but he could appreciate it—when it was good. River Hill was located smack in the middle of California's Russian River appellation, and it stood to reason if an award-winning restaurant stocked the stuff, this one would be.

He swirled the glass and inhaled. Right away, he

picked up the musty aroma some pinots were known for, followed by hints of black cherry and mint. *So far so good.* He took a small sip, and his taste buds fired. "Feck, that's good," he said, smacking his lips together appreciatively.

Noah smiled, and then filled both their glasses. "It should be. It won a double gold this summer."

"Nice."

Noah nodded. "Yeah, it was. Especially since my dad took home the same award five years in a row before me."

"Ah," Iain said, taking another drink. "You know exactly what I'm talking about, then."

"Maybe not exactly," Noah mused, holding his glass up to the light and inspecting the 'legs' that snaked down the side when he tilted it. "But enough to know you've probably got an uphill battle in front of you."

Iain exhaled. That was putting it mildly. Every time he thought he'd made progress with his family, they'd read some article or hear some rumor that would have them expressing concern for the venture. Some days, he felt like Sisyphus pushing that damn boulder up the hill, only to watch it roll all the way back down again. It sometimes made him wonder if it was all worth it. But then he'd spent the holidays with his family and seen his two older brothers leading near-identical lives and known that it was.

He loved his family, and he loved Ireland, but Iain wanted … well, he wanted something more. He knew that made him sound ungrateful, but he was the third son, and he'd always known he'd have to forge his own path or be stuck following in his brothers' footsteps, never quite getting the chance to be his own man.

"Yeah," Iain agreed, taking another sip and savoring the complex flavors. "The latest battle is about the name and the label. Even if I can prove this is a viable venture, they don't want to deviate too far from the traditional branding. I get it; everyone knows the Brennan name and recognizes the label. But this isn't Brennan whiskey—I mean it is, obviously—but it's different casks, new blends, totally new flavor profiles. Essentially, really experimental stuff the traditionalists in my family don't understand."

"Okay, now, that's *exactly* like what I went through with my dad." Noah pointed at him. "He offered to let me make my own wine, but it all had to be under his label. I could have my name on it—in smaller font, obviously— but it still had to be his."

"Exactly!" Iain shot back, gratified to have found someone who understood what he was going through. Someone, it seemed, who'd come out the other end successful. "This can't be 'Brennan's Blended Whiskey' or whatever they want to call it. This is like nothing we've ever done before. It has to be totally new and fresh—and that includes the name and the label. Only every graphic designer I know is on my dad's payroll, and the ones I've tried to find elsewhere have been rubbish" He sighed and rolled his eyes. "If I see one more watercolor barley chaff I'm going to fucking scream."

Noah rubbed his chin thoughtfully, then twisted the bottle of wine around so the label faced Iain. "What do you think of this?"

Iain studied it for a few seconds. The colors were bold, the font eye catching while still being easy to read, and the overall design strong and masculine without being too in-your-face. It was a great match for the man who'd produced the wine within. "I like it. Why?"

"My friend's an artist who does graphic design on the side. She does all my labels. I'd be happy to put you guys in touch."

Iain considered the offer. He wasn't getting anywhere with the design team back home, and he hadn't stumbled upon a design here he liked well enough to put it on the bottles he'd brought with him. He knew the fact that it looked like he was peddling hooch wasn't doing him any favors. If he wanted to get distributors in the U.S. on board with the new brand, his whiskey needed to look the part. And that meant getting his shit together and hiring someone who'd produce a beautiful label that would stand out from the competition. Noah's offer just might be the lifesaver he needed.

"Yeah, sure. That'd be grand. Does she have a card you can give me?"

"I don't think I have one on hand, but I can set up a meeting for you, if you'd like. She's local."

"Perfect. Let me know the time and date and I'll be there." Iain shook the other man's hand again. "I can't thank you enough."

Noah grinned at him. "Oh, I bet you can."

5

"A client?" Naomi balanced her phone with her chin. She'd managed to answer it with her wrist, since her hands were covered in the grey slime of wet clay. "I don't know, Noah, I'm pretty busy. I told you about Z Gallery, right?"

"At least three times." Noah's dry tone came clearly through the phone.

"I've gotten two of the three exclusive pieces done, but the last one's giving me some trouble," she said. The misshapen lump of clay on her work table reproached her silently. Her creativity was quickly approaching burnout after the sheer amount of work she'd been doing lately.

"Maybe a change of pace would do you good."

"I don't know if I have time for a change of pace."

"He seems like a nice guy. Beverage industry dudes need to stick together, and he said those new labels you did for me were the sort of thing he was looking for."

"Uh-huh." She traced a finger through the clay, drawing squiggly lines and curlicues over the lump.

"Didn't that craft beer job I sent you pay for those new windows in your studio?"

"Yes," she admitted grudgingly.

"Nay, you have a perfectly good degree in graphic design and a reasonably successful company with leads falling in your lap. You might as well use it."

"It's not *art*, Noah."

"Just take a break from whatever weird clay ritual you're doing and meet him, please? I told him I'd set it up."

"Look at you, making promises. Who would have thunk it?"

"Funny girl. Speaking of promises, Angelica will be back from filming next week. Want to have dinner with us?"

"Why, what are you trying to convince her of?"

"To get married." Noah didn't even try to pretend he didn't have ulterior motives.

Naomi snorted a laugh. "You think having your former sex buddy over for dinner is going to convince your girlfriend to marry you?"

"No, I think one of my best friends is going to convince her for me. Come on, you know Angelica loves you. You're part of the 'Noah Package' I'm trying to sell."

"Ugh, keep your Noah Package away from me."

"I'll put you down as a yes, then."

"Fine. What day?"

"Not sure yet. I'll get back to you on that. And on the meeting."

"If I must."

Maybe Noah was right, and she did need a break. She could definitely use a new computer, and the advance from Z Gallery wasn't going to cut it after the rest of her bills got paid.

"You're literally an artist, and NK Designs is the most imaginative name you could come up with?" Max looked at the business card she'd handed him, brows wrinkled dubiously.

"Words aren't really my favorite medium," Naomi said. "Somebody once told me it's better to use your initials than your full name, because people have all kinds of gender biases when it comes to female business owners. So, I went with it."

Max shrugged. "I guess I can't really argue. My name's Max and I own a restaurant called Frankie's."

She grinned. "You wouldn't argue anyway. Drop me an email with what you're thinking about for your menu redesign and I'll get you a rough draft." She was killing two birds with one stone. Max had mentioned getting his menus redesigned a few weeks ago, and since she'd taken Noah's advice to heart, she'd had him schedule her meeting with his new friend at Frankie's so she could also talk to Max about the menus. They'd agreed on a price— the friends and family discount, of course—and now she was headed to the booth in the corner, the leather folder she kept her design portfolio in tucked under her arm.

She'd rather devote all of her time to her clay, but she wasn't yet a big enough name to not need the additional income. Much as she hated to admit it, putting her degree to use made sense, so when Noah had first asked her to design his labels, she'd taken the time to set up NK Designs as a legitimate business—tax license and all. Her mother would have been shocked, if she'd ever asked about Naomi's career enough to learn where her money came from.

Naomi settled into the booth and picked up the menu on the table, perusing it absently. She already knew what she was going to order, but she wanted to take a look at the layout to see what changes she'd be making. Absorbed in her mental note-taking, she didn't pay attention to the other customers. Noah had said he'd make the introductions, so she didn't look up until she heard his voice.

"There you are." He loomed over the table. Noah Bradstone was a tall man, and solidly built. His friend was pretty much hidden behind him.

She put on her professional smile. "Hi. Thanks for—" She stopped dead as Noah moved aside, revealing the man who'd been standing in his wake. "Iain?"

The same man she'd had some of the most incredible sex of her life with three months ago was staring back at her, equally surprised. "Naomi?"

She drank in the sight of him, clothed in a simple grey henley and jeans that fit far more perfectly than any pair of pants had a right to. His beard was a little less perfectly trimmed than it had been the night they'd met, and his hair stood up in slightly more spiky patterns. But the blue eyes were the same, the laugh lines crinkling in a welcoming smile.

She forced her eyes away before they could travel appreciatively all the way down his body. She didn't need to know exactly how well those jeans were cupping the areas she was intimately familiar with. She looked over at Noah, who was smirking. Typical.

"Is this the friend you wanted me to meet? I didn't know you knew each other." She managed to keep her tone professional.

"I didn't realize *you* did," Noah said. "When could you possibly have met?"

"Um, at the Founders' Ball a few months ago."

He winced. "Oh, right. Sorry."

"You were distracted," she said with an airy wave of her hand. "Although Angelica told me some stuff about an elevator that was very intriguing."

"Never mind." He paused, eyes narrowing. "I talked to my mom last week, and she said you didn't stay for the closing toasts." He looked back and forth between Naomi and Iain, and she could practically see the wheels turning in his head.

"Never mind yourself," she said quickly.

He shrugged. "I'll just call your brother."

"Do it and I'll call your mother and invite her to come down here and plan your wedding."

He rolled his eyes. "If you can get Angelica to agree to a wedding, you can call anybody you want. But I'll leave you two to get acquainted. Or do I mean re-acquainted?" He walked in the direction of the bar, chortling the whole way.

"I'm sorry," Naomi said. "I've known him since I was seven. Sometimes I think he hasn't aged since then."

"It's all right." Iain folded himself into the booth, the cushion squeaking quietly under him.

"He should have just given you my card, or just emailed both of us." Naomi rolled her eyes. "He can't resist a prank, apparently." Noah knew her 'type' perfectly well, since he'd been one of them before he met Angelica. He probably thought he was setting her up on a blind date. Now that he was in love, he wanted everyone else to settle down, too. Even though he knew her opinion on *that* topic perfectly well. If she could have rolled her eyes further back in her head, she would have.

"I'll bet that goes over well at home."

Naomi chuckled. "He has calmed down a lot since he and Angelica got together. But she travels half the time to film her show, so I guess he has to take it out on the rest of us. He once replaced all of Max's shower gel with olive oil."

"Joke was on him," Max said as he arrived at their table and set a plate of tacos down in front of Iain. "I didn't even notice. Here's your favorite."

"Are you sure the joke's not on you, for using shower gel in the first place?" Iain asked with a grin.

"Gets into the nooks and crannies better," Max responded blithely. "Naomi, you want me to commit crimes against lettuce-kind for you?"

"Yes, please." She noticed Iain's raised eyebrow and explained as Max departed. "He leaves the roasted red peppers off of the salad I usually order for me."

"You're a regular, eh?"

She nodded toward his plate. "Looks like you are, too."

"I've only been here a couple of days, but I'm smart enough to know a good thing when I stumble into it." He glanced from the tacos to her and raised an eyebrow.

She felt herself growing warm. The double meaning was obvious. "I, ah, brought my portfolio."

"Yeah?" He was waiting to eat until her food arrived, she realized as he pulled the folder across the table. *How polite.*

"Organized by format," she said, trying to put her business face back on. "There's digital assets, print ones, and a couple of full branding packages that included everything from logo design to web graphics plus business cards, flyers, and product packaging."

He flipped through the pages, nodding. "This is all really nice." He looked up at her. "I really liked the label Noah showed me. The wine?"

"Yeah, that's actually in here." She reached across the table and flipped a few pages forward, then tapped the sheet. "See, there's actually a progression. I've been designing his labels for several years now, so you can see how the brand has grown and shifted a bit while still retaining its core identity."

"How long did you say you've known him?"

"Since I was seven. Our parents are good friends."

If this was a business meeting, she probably shouldn't get too personal. And if this was going to be a repeat of the night of the gala, she definitely didn't want to mention that she and Noah had been sleeping together for years—at least until he'd met Angelica.

Naomi had liked the former actress from the moment she first met her, and she'd done her best to push Noah into realizing that his feelings were real. The little friends-with-benefits thing they'd had going hadn't been worth giving up on finding what he was really looking for. She was just glad he'd realized it in time.

And she was even more glad that Angelica had turned out to be the sort of woman who didn't particularly care about Noah's past sex life. They'd spent many an evening cheerfully roasting him over a few glasses of his own wine, as he'd rolled his eyes and pretended to be offended.

Realizing where her thoughts were going, Naomi tried to refocus. Iain was here on business, and she never slept with a one-night-stand twice. It only led to people thinking she was interested in commitment. She'd learned that lesson early on. She didn't know which was worse—men thinking they were entitled to her time, or her mother thinking she should give it to them. Either way, her policy had stood her in good stead for years now, and she wasn't throwing it all away for Iain … no matter how gloriously big his hands were. Or other things.

"What are you looking for?" She leveled her gaze at Iain and hoped it was steady. It was hard to conduct a business meeting with somebody you'd enthusiastically fucked without making everything seem like an invitation. She'd never actually been in this situation before.

His lips tilted in a tiny smile. "I'm not entirely sure."

Well, that wasn't helpful. She was saved from further trips down Double Entendre Lane by Max's reappearance. "Here." He plunked her plate down in front of her. "I hope you know you're ruining the flavor profile."

"Roasted peppers don't have a flavor profile. They're just slimy."

"Ugh. Naomi, for somebody who grew up extremely fancy, you're very boring."

"Shows how much you know." She stuck her tongue out at Max. "I'm very exciting. Do you know what's not exciting? Roasted peppers."

He threw his hands up in the air and stalked away, muttering something about missing components and mouthfeel.

She grinned at Iain. "He hates it when people make substitutions."

"I've got a mate back home who feels the same way," he said with a laugh. "Something about how everything on the plate is supposed to work in harmony when you put it all on a fork together."

"I could probably just pick the peppers out, but it's much more fun to annoy him."

"Who could blame you?" Iain grinned at her and picked up a taco, taking a healthy bite.

She dug into her own salad. "I'm so glad we agree." Now if only she could get her body to agree with her mind that leaping across the table and ripping his clothes off probably *wasn't* a good idea, she'd be set.

6

Iain couldn't stop staring at Naomi's mouth, remembering all the wicked ways she'd used it on him months before. He was having a hard time concentrating on what she was saying about the work she did for companies like his, but that was okay—flipping through her portfolio, he'd already decided to hire her. He'd seen the finished product with Noah's labels, and everything she'd shown him in the last few minutes put her well ahead of the designers he'd spoken with previously. It was a no-brainer, really.

Setting his plate to the side, he took a long pull on his iced tea. He twisted the portfolio around and pushed it toward Naomi. "I like the look and feel of these." He studied the upside-down images for a few more seconds before dragging his gaze back up to find Naomi chewing delicately on her bottom lip.

She dropped her gaze to the images he'd pointed to, examined them for a few seconds, and then raised her eyes again. All business now, she said, "That vintage-modern look is very on-trend. It harkens back to a time when goods weren't as disposable as they are now, so people subconsciously equate it with quality. The use of strong, masculine fonts also works well for the spirits industry."

Quality. That was something Iain's father understood, even if he didn't think his youngest son did. "I'm looking for something that will satisfy my dad and brothers, since I need them to sign off on this venture. But I'd love to hear how you can incorporate some of my sister into the design as well. She's the genius behind the whiskey."

"Oh, I hadn't realized you had a sister."

The only reason Iain knew she had a brother was because he'd met the man. But once they'd left the ball, he and Naomi hadn't spent the night studying their respective family trees. But perhaps it was time they actually *did* get to know one another? If he was going to use River Hill as his base of operations, they would run into each other from time to time. Coming back here after his trips up and down the coast was sounding better and better. And if he could persuade Naomi to take him on as a client, they'd be spending a *lot* more time together. At least he assumed that's how it worked. This was all new to him.

Truth be known, he wanted this spirited, unique woman to know him. The real him. Even if it was just for a while. "Two older brothers—Braden and Fionn—and my sister, Maeve. We're Irish twins."

"What's that?"

"She was born on January first, and I was born on December thirtieth."

Naomi's eyes bugged out, and she flattened her palms on the tabletop. "In the same year?" she asked, her face displaying her horror at the concept.

Iain chuckled. For as strained as his relationship with his father had been lately, he couldn't deny the man was madly in love with his mother—even after all these years. Personally, he didn't think the whole "until death do us part" thing was for him, but if he were to ever settle down with someone, he hoped he'd be as mad for her as his parents were for each other. "The old man can't keep his hands off my mother. Half the time, I don't know whether to be happy my parents are still together or disgusted by how blissful they are."

Her brows furrowed, and Iain could tell she was working out the math. "How is that even possible?" She shuddered and shook her head as if to chase away whatever thought had taken up residence there.

"Different times, I guess," he answered with a shrug before hailing a waitress for a refill of his iced tea. "If I'm going to think about sex, it's not my parents I want to be picturing."

He let his gaze fall to Naomi's lips before dragging his eyes back up to meet hers. She looked adorably flustered, and he wondered if she was picturing sex now. Specifically, the sex they'd had. The sex he hoped to have again in the not-too-distant future, if he was honest.

"Oh right, got it. Yes, of course."

"Relax, Naomi. I'm just taking the piss."

She groaned and raised a hand to her forehead. "And now I'm picturing your hand wrapped around your dick, and I'm sorry, but that is really not fair." She leveled a frustrated glare at him. "You're making it very hard to be professional right now."

Iain let his lips hitch to the side with a smirk, and he saw Naomi's eyes go wide with understanding. Her face reddened, and she pointed at him. "Stop it. You stop it right now, Iain …"

His first name dangled into the long pause, and he watched her visibly struggle to come up with his surname. Now he was fighting a full-on grin. "You don't remember it, do you?"

Her eyes flashed with something that might have been either guilt or annoyance, and she chewed her lip again. God, he loved it when she did that. It reminded him of the face she made when she was close to coming. "I don't suppose it's Jameson?"

"No, sweetheart. I'm not a Jameson." Iain knew he should be nice and just tell her his damn name, but he derived a perverse sense of satisfaction watching her squirm. To be honest, he couldn't remember if they'd even ever exchanged last names that night. But this was too much fun not to continue.

Her eyes scanned the restaurant, and he watched as she tried to see across the room to the bar. "Sorry. Max is all out. He says a new shipment arrives tomorrow." Of course, Frankie's stocked Brennan's.

She slapped her napkin down. "Okay, fine. You caught me. I can't remember your damn last name."

He smiled and leaned forward, reducing the space that separated them. "Ask me nicely."

Naomi gritted her teeth. "What is your last name, Iain?"

He reached across the table and rubbed his thumb over the top of her delicate-looking hand—the one he knew from experience was anything but. She'd raked her nails down his back the first time he'd made her come, and then she'd gouged the plaster in the wall above the headboard the second time. Her hands were strong and capable, and he desperately wanted to feel them on his skin again.

"How about this? You take me back to your place, and I'll spend the afternoon making you scream it?"

Naomi opened her mouth to speak, then immediately closed it. She tilted her head to the side and studied him for a couple of seconds. "Here's the deal," she said eventually, pulling her hand away and crossing her arms over her chest. "I don't sleep with people I work with. Call me old-fashioned, but I never mix business with pleasure. You can either hire me to do your labels, or you can come back to my house and fuck my brains out. Your choice." She finished by raising one elegant eyebrow at him.

Having seen her work, Iain knew what he wanted his labels to look like. But he also knew no woman had made his pulse quicken and his blood run hot and furious through his veins the way this one did. There really was no choice at all.

He slid from the booth and reached into his back pocket. Pulling out his wallet, he dropped two twenty-dollar bills on the table—enough to cover their lunches, plus a hefty tip.

"Will losing my business impact your bottom line?"

Naomi smiled up at him and licked her lips. "Not even remotely."

"Then let's get out of here." He turned and made his way to the door, knowing deep in his bones—and elsewhere—she'd be right behind him.

Twenty agonizingly long minutes later, they stumbled through the door of a charming bungalow several blocks from the restaurant, their limbs twined around each other and their mouths fused together.

Iain kicked the door closed and hoisted Naomi up by her ass, her long, lithe legs wrapping around his waist before he backed her against it. He kissed a path down her jaw to reach the pulse beating violently in her neck. He sucked the dancing point into his mouth and then, moving lower, tongued the frilly lace edge of her bra.

"Bedroom?" he asked against her soft skin.

"Down the hall." Naomi tugged on his belt buckle and then popped the button of his jeans before lowering the zipper. Reaching her hand down the front of his trousers, she cupped him over his boxer briefs and squeezed.

Iain groaned and dropped his head back to stare up at the ceiling while she continued stroking him. "Fuck, that feels fantastic." He blew out a long breath, thankful he hadn't misremembered how talented Naomi was with her hands.

"Then this will feel even better." She slid down the length of him to land on her knees, lowering his clothes as she went.

Iain's head fell forward when she wrapped her slender fingers around his cock and angled it toward her mouth, her eyes trained on him the entire time. She licked him from root to tip, and with a hum of approval, swirled her tongue around his crown like it was a Teddy's 99 on a hot, summer day. He'd never look at ice cream cones the same way again. "Christ, woman."

Naomi flashed him a wicked grin and then took him deep. Those were the last words out of his mouth until he came with a shout.

With his hands flattened against the door and his chest heaving in and out, he stared down at the beautiful woman on her knees in front of him. "You're fucking perfect."

"I know." Naomi pushed to her feet, then grabbed his hand and led him through the foyer, past the eclectically-decorated living room, and into a darkened room dominated by a wrought iron four poster bed. She kicked off her shoes, yanked her pale blue blouse off over her head, slid her trousers down her long legs, and then climbed naked on top of the fluffy white duvet.

Iain eyed her greedily as she rested against the enormous pile of pillows at her back. Then she trailed her fingers down the expanse of her creamy white skin until she reached the small slope of her belly. He watched with rapt attention as she traced a light pattern over the flesh there until goosebumps sprouted.

And then they coasted lower … and lower … and lower."And now you're going to return the favor."

Hell yeah, he was.

7

So maybe it was a *two*-night stand. Naomi rolled over lazily and stared at Iain, who was sleeping peacefully in her giant bed, his limbs sprawled loosely as he lay in the same position he'd collapsed in after their last round. His breathing was slow and even, the hair of his beard underneath his bottom lip waving gently with each exhale. Her thighs had felt that same hair a few times last night, and she reached down to lightly stroke the reddened skin.

Two nights with the same man probably weren't going to kill her, unless it was death by orgasm. A distinct possibility, given the events of the night before. She grinned. She probably shouldn't have issued that little ultimatum at Frankie's, but she didn't see how she could work with Iain *and* sleep with him. And given a choice between the two, she was glad he'd picked the second one. She was sorry he'd have to find another designer, but she had the gig redesigning Max's menu to generate some extra income.

She thought of her studio upstairs and the work she had to complete in order to claim payment from the gallery. Instead of the dragging weariness she'd been feeling for the last several days, she felt… excited. Creative. Interested.

Could it be?

"Yessss," she hissed to herself. She glanced at Iain again. He was still sleeping peacefully. Maybe all she'd needed to get her artistic mojo back was some rest and relaxation. Emphasis on the relaxation part—not so much the rest, given how little she'd slept last night. She flexed her fingers. Her muscles felt loose and warm. She let one leg dangle over the edge of the bed, then scooted over an inch. No response from the sleeping collection of muscles next to her. She slid further toward the edge, then out of the bed entirely when his breathing didn't change.

She found a pair of yoga pants and a tank top lying in a pile next to her dresser and pulled them on as silently as she could manage. A quick trip to the bathroom, then to the kitchen to pull out the cold-brewed coffee in the fridge, mixing it with almond milk. She left an empty glass out on the counter in case Iain wanted some. Finally, she headed upstairs.

As she opened the door at the top of the stairs, she felt her whole body start to tingle with excitement. It was going to be a good day; she could feel it in her fingertips. Forgetting completely about the man sleeping in her bed downstairs, she set her coffee down on her work table and headed to the clay cabinet to pull out her materials.

When she'd bought this house, it had been in need of some serious renovation. The downstairs work had been simple: refinish the floors, fix some plaster, and replace the sink in the bathroom. She'd kept the vintage kitchen, though she'd replaced the countertops. Upstairs was a different story. There had been three small bedrooms, a bizarrely large landing at the top of the stairs, and a bathroom tucked under the eaves of the roof. After conferring with her contractors and paying an architect an exorbitant amount of money to make sure it was safe, she'd knocked down every single wall. The entire upstairs was now a bright, airy studio. She'd kept the bathroom, though she'd replaced everything about it and switched the tub to a small walk-in shower to save space. She wasn't bathing up here, but it was nice to be able to get clay dust out of her hair occasionally.

Her brother had come out to see it when the renovations were complete, bringing some of her old pieces of sculpture from their parents' storage unit. He'd muttered darkly about resale value. Nobody would want to buy a house with only one bedroom, but she didn't care. She'd fallen in love with River Hill the second she'd visited the town, back when Noah had bought his vineyard here more than ten years ago.

When she'd finally decided to settle down—stop roving up and down the coast as an artist-in-residence anywhere that would take her—the choice of where to live had been obvious. River Hill was close enough to San Francisco to easily get back for the events her parents insisted she attend, but far enough away to keep her family at bay otherwise. Plus, she'd gotten a great deal on this house, and she was pretty sure her property values went up every time Max got nominated for a

James Beard award or Noah's wine won yet another award.

She chuckled. *Property values!* If her mother could hear her now.

She hummed quietly as she worked the clay to loosen it. She felt warm, relaxed, creative. Like she could finally see the images in the clay again, the ones hidden inside screaming to be let out by her hands and her tools. With the ease of long practice, she slid a second brick of clay onto her table and began to alternate her kneading. When the two chunks were flexible enough, she'd combine them. This piece was going to be big. She would shape the basic form of the sculpture first—a large egg-like thing built around a stability rod with some assistance from structural wire—then let it dry. Later, she'd move on to the carving portion of the proceedings: her favorite. She loved scraping away tiny layers of clay to find the art underneath.

Two hours later, she sat back from the table with a satisfied sigh. "There." She narrowed her eyes. "Wait." She leaned forward and used the back edge of her hand to create a shallow, curving divot along the length of the shape. "Much better."

"What is it?" Iain's voice came from the doorway.

She whipped around and discovered him leaning against the doorframe, clad in the same clothes he'd worn yesterday, but with hair visibly wet from a shower. He raised the glass she'd left out for him. "Thanks for the coffee."

"Oh. Um, you're welcome." She blinked at him, trying to bring herself back to the real world.

"Did I interrupt? I'm sorry."

"No, I—" She frowned at him. "Wait, how long have you been there?"

He grinned. "Not too long. About twenty minutes. You seemed busy, so I watched."

She didn't usually let people come up here at all, let alone watch her work. But she hadn't even noticed him. Either she'd been in some kind of creative trance or he'd been incredibly quiet. Maybe both.

She moved automatically to clean up her mess, gathering the plastic wrap and the boxes the clay had come in, as well as a few stray, drying crumbs of the stuff, before tossing them all into a large garbage can in the corner. "I, um, didn't want to wake you."

Aside from Noah, she'd never had sex in River Hill. It was her sanctuary, the place she did her most creative work. Even he'd only been in her house a few times, and only in her bed once—on a night they'd had too much wine to go anywhere else. And he'd had the courtesy to creep out silently in the morning before she got up, since he generally woke at some bizarre early hour of the morning to go and do farm-like things at the vineyard.

But here was Iain. In her house. In her studio! He'd slept in her bed! What was she doing? He was watching her steadily as she cleaned, sipping his coffee slowly but not making any move to approach her.

She folded up the faded canvas she used to cover her work table and told herself to relax. It was just Iain. He was nice, he did extremely good work with his hands, and he wasn't staying. He'd need to go looking for another designer for his labels, for one thing.

She pasted a smile on her face and turned to him. "All done."

He raised an eyebrow. "You never answered me."

"What?"

He nodded toward her piece, now drying on the rack next to the work table. "What is it?"

"Oh." She stared at it, feeling awkward. Nobody had come to look at her work in progress since she'd been an artist-in-residence and it had been part of the requirements of the position to allow studio tours. She'd never done her best work that way. But the rent had been free. "I'm actually not entirely sure yet." She smiled fondly at the blank shape as it sat there, waiting for her to sharpen its edges. "But it's going to be good."

She shooed Iain back downstairs before he could ask any more questions, not wanting to disrupt the bubbling creative energy she could feel still lurking in the studio. The clay would need at least a day to dry before she could touch it, and she didn't want whatever mojo she'd finally gotten back to disappear again.

She froze at the bottom of the stairs, one foot in midair, as a new thought occurred to her. Was *Iain* her lucky charm? She winced internally even as she thought it. He was Irish; he probably wouldn't appreciate the phrasing. She shook her head. It was impossible, anyway. That sort of thing wasn't real. Art came from inside the artist, taking inspiration from the world around them. It didn't come from sex. If it did, she'd have produced a lot more sculptures by now. She grinned as she bounced down the last step.

"So what's next?" Iain met her in the kitchen.

"Breakfast?" Naomi was starving. "I didn't have anything but coffee before I went up." Breakfast with somebody she'd slept with! She was trying all kinds of new things today. Maybe she was finally growing as a person like her family wanted her to.

"I meant with your sculpture," he said, waving his arm vaguely towards the ceiling. "But I could eat." His grin made laugh lines appear in his cheeks around his beard. She liked it.

"Oh!" She laughed. "The clay has to dry for a day or so. Then I'll carve it."

"And you don't know what you'll be carving it into?"

She shrugged. "I've got a vague idea. But the details are inside the clay." She moved to the pantry. "I've got, um, granola. And some of those breakfast cracker things."

"Not a bacon and eggs type of girl?" He tilted his head towards her fridge.

She reached back to pull it open to show him its contents. "More like orange juice and an occasional yogurt. Sorry." If she wasn't working in the studio in the mornings, she was usually practicing yoga. And nobody liked doing yoga on a full stomach.

"I'll trouble you for a bowl of granola," he said. "And then I'm afraid I've got to be on my way."

She let out a long, slow breath. There it was. She wasn't sure whether to be glad or annoyed that he was as ready to scamper out of her house as she was to toss him. Breakfast with a guy was broadening her horizons enough. She was already starting to get anxious about when he would start demanding more of her time. She had art to create. Hopefully, he had plenty of his own work to do.

"Got a lot on your plate today?" She handed him the box of granola.

"A conference call with my father and the CEO—also known as my brother." He winced. "I was going to tell them I'd found a designer to work with, but ...." He poured himself a bowl, then peered up at her with wide puppy-dog eyes. "Don't suppose you'd—"

She held up a hand. "You picked, my friend."

He snorted. "I'll wear you down."

She smiled at him sweetly. "I'll give you some names." She didn't need the money enough to break her rules. She'd made them for good reasons. And she wasn't about to tempt herself by letting him hang around. "Eat your granola."

"Mmm. Crunchy."

She let out a huff of laughter and dug into her own cereal.

After Iain left, with a couple of kisses and a few more hints about hiring her, she settled down at her computer, an old workhorse of a Mac that was taking longer and longer to fire up the layout and design software she used. She sighed. Maybe she *should* do Iain's labels. She really did need a new computer.

She shook her head. There were other ways to make money. There was a request in her inbox now, actually, from a local beauty blogger who wanted a new logo designed. And of course there was Max's new menus. Which she should really focus on, instead of thinking about last night and the way Iain had moved with her, under her, over her, and inside her. She shivered. *Best to get it out of your system, girl.*

She'd had two nights with him. That would be enough. Wouldn't it?

8

There were no words to describe how mind blowing his night with Naomi had been, but as Iain stared at his laptop, he briefly wondered if all those orgasms had been worth his sanity. Because even though he'd been explicit about what he was looking for from the graphic designer he'd spoken with after returning from Naomi's, yet *another* watercolor wheat chaff was on his screen. At this rate, he'd be showing up at his next sales call like some snake oil salesman, pulling an unlabeled bottle out of his leather satchel and trying to convince his potential buyer it wasn't complete swill.

With a defeated sigh, he pushed the laptop away and raised his eyes to the ceiling. He'd gone without a cigarette for almost a year, but now he craved one—desperately. Instead, he reached blindly for the bottle of bourbon on the table next to him and raised it to his lips. Since he'd begun hanging out with Max and Noah, he'd taken to drinking the stuff. His father would probably foam at the mouth if he knew Iain hadn't had a drop of Irish whiskey in days, but that was just too damn bad.

As if that thought conjured the old man himself, Iain's phone rang, a picture of his father alerting him to an incoming video call. Before answering, he scanned the room to make sure it was clean and presentable and that the bottle he'd been drinking from was hidden from view.

"Iain." His father leaned forward, his eyes squinted as if inspecting his son for some flaw. His jaw ticked, and he settled back in his office chair, crossing his arms over his chest.

Clearly, he'd found something about his son's appearance he didn't approve of. Inwardly, Iain made a bet with himself. If his dad complained about his beard, he'd finish off the bourbon and order takeout. If, instead, he focused on Iain's charming, albeit small, room at The Oakwell Inn, he'd head over to Frankie's for a plate of tacos. Either way, he'd end the night on a positive note.

"Your beard is too long," the other man barked as Iain's hands itched to reach for the bourbon. "No one's going to take you seriously if you look like a hippie." Iain bit his tongue—literally—as his father continued. "It's sloppy."

Cathal Brennan had never worn a beard a day in his life and didn't understand why his youngest son chose to. Aside from not liking how it looked, Iain's father also frequently remarked on how aggravating it must be always having things caught in it. Iain's eating abilities were somewhat beyond that of a toddler, and he wasn't carting around bits of his lunch on his face all the damn time, but it wasn't worth arguing. At first, he'd let his fashionable stubble grow into a neatly trimmed beard as part of a small rebellion against the tyranny of his father's rules, but once he'd become accustomed to it, he'd decided to keep it.

Now, he ran his hand over the bristles, testing its length and softness. He'd found a new clove-scented beard oil in a shop down the street from Frankie's and liked how it made the hair on his face both feel and smell. "I'll take that under advisement. In the meantime, to what do I owe the pleasure?"

"I told you I'd call this week to discuss where you're at with lining up customers for Brennan's Small Batch."

Iain chose to ignore the name his father had given Maeve's whiskey. They'd discussed it at length, and he knew until his sister and he wrestled control of the whiskey from the hands of their brothers and father, the man wouldn't budge. Instead, he focused on the timing of the call. "You said you'd call on Thursday; today is Tuesday."

"No, I said Tuesday. You need to do a better job remembering your commitments. You should write them down instead of relying on that phone of yours to keep your schedule."

For a split second Iain contemplated ending the call without saying goodbye. There was only so much abuse a man could take, and he was quickly reaching the end of his rope. If it wouldn't destroy his mother, he sometimes considered severing all ties with the old man. Iain knew his father loved him, but he didn't think the man actually *liked* him that much.

Iain pinched the bridge of his nose and closed his eyes. "What did you want to discuss?"

"How many customers have you lined up since our last conversation?"

Iain blew out a breath and fixed his gaze on the swirls and dips of the purple silk curtains that framed a view of the vine-covered hillside beyond. "Ten." Which was about twenty less than he'd been aiming for this month. The overall goal had been to secure one hundred bars and restaurants that would be willing to serve Whitman's Revival—the name he and Maeve had agreed on—by the time his six months in the U.S. were up, but so far Iain had fallen well short of that target, and the realization stung.

If he were launching the expression in Ireland, he would have had that many customers lined up within a week, even without labels on the bottles. Breaking into the U.S. markets without relying on his family's PR machine backing the venture was proving more difficult than he'd anticipated. Maybe it had been a naive dream, but he'd figured with such a sizable focus on craft distillers in the States, customers would welcome him— and his superior liquid—with open arms.

Iain wasn't being arrogant; what his brilliant sister had created (with a bit of his input, of course) was remarkable whiskey. A fifteen-year-old single malt matured in bourbon barrels before being finished in Pedro Ximenez sherry puncheons was some of the best whiskey he had tasted in years. With a nose that recalled relaxing in an oak-lined library, the scent of a wood fire blazing in the hearth while you sipped mulled wine and snacked on fresh gingerbread, Whitman's lingered on the tongue with silky notes of sticky toffee pudding, candied fruits, cinnamon, and nutmeg. To Iain's mind, it was Christmas in a glass, and it was unlike anything anyone in Ireland was currently producing.

"That's not going to cut it, son."

"I know," he groaned. *Trust me, I know.* "But I've still got sixty days to line up the remaining forty customers, and I have some ideas that I think are going to work. I met with a designer—"

"I told you; you should use ours. They know Brennan's branding and what works for the label."

"We talked about this, dad. We don't want to launch another Brennan's whiskey. What Maeve has done is so different from anything our family has ever put out. We want it to stand on its own."

"While relying on my connections for barrels and using my facility for storage." His father snorted. "But you and Maeve keep telling yourself you're doing this on your own."

Iain bit back the retort that rested bitterly on the tip of his tongue. His dad might be the chairman of Brennan Family Distillers, one of the only independently owned and operated whiskey brands left in the country, but he didn't own the company outright. Thanks to Iain's great-great-great grandfather, every male Brennan was given a share of the company immediately upon his birth. A fact his sister, a better distiller than any of his brothers or uncles could ever claim to be, bemoaned almost daily. The patriarchy wasn't kind to female Brennans. But since Iain owned approximately two percent of the company, and the Whitman's barrels took up significantly less than two percent of floor space in the warehouse, he had no ethical qualms about using a Brennan facility for storage.

Gripping the roots of his hair tight in his fist, Iain kept his voice as even as he could. "Is this the part of our conversation where I remind you that I own two percent of Brennan's, and that technically speaking, you're only a majority shareholder—not the only one?" It was probably a mistake to poke the bear, but he didn't seem to have a choice.

Iain's father bristled visibly, and his face flushed red. "If so, this must be the part of the conversation where I remind you that you have sixty days left to make a success of this harebrained scheme. If you can't, I expect you back at your desk in Dublin, or I might be forced to find someone else to take over your job."

With those last snapped words, his father abruptly ended the call, leaving Iain to stew over the old threat hanging over his head. The threat that kept him up at night, wondering if he was fooling himself … if he actually had what it took to make a go of this.

Iain wasn't too proud to admit he'd gotten his job because of *who* he was, but he'd also attended university and done an intensive internship in London. He had the education to back up his ideas. And it was his idea and hard work that had earned the tasting room an award for being the top tourist attraction in Dublin. *He'd* done that; not his father … and certainly not his brothers. t pissed him off that regardless of his success, they had the power to make him doubt himself.

Fucking imposter syndrome, he thought as he pushed off the chair and paced the floor—what little there was of it..

He loved the Oakwell Inn, but his room was the smallest one, the majority of the floor space taken up by the plush queen bed and an antique bureau. With a quick sweep of his eyes over the space, he acknowledged he couldn't stay there much longer. Landing at Noah's girlfriend's B&B that first day had been a stroke of good luck, but the costs were adding up. Since he now planned on camping out in River Hill for two more months, he needed to find a less expensive, more permanent place to stay. The town's central location and artisan population made it a good base of operations for his plan, but a pricy bed and breakfast wasn't really in the budget.

Unbidden, his mind flashed to Naomi's cute little bungalow at the edge of town. Not that he was thinking of asking her if he could stay there—he liked the woman just fine, and her bed *had* been incredibly comfortable, but that was taking things a bit far. No, what he needed was a little cottage of his own. Someplace he could stretch out and think. Someplace he didn't have to feel guilty for coming in late or walking in on the housekeeper folding his drawers. Somewhere he could invite a certain dark-haired beauty to spend the night if he wanted.

But before that could happen, he'd need to convince her to see him again. They hadn't discussed their two amazing hook-ups, but Iain knew a person who wanted to keep things casual when he saw one—mostly because Naomi's attitude thus far mirrored his own exactly. No promises of tomorrow, no declarations of intent … just incredible, toe-curling sex followed by a "see you when I see you" mentality. They weren't friends, not exactly, and yet for all of his carefree approach to relationships, he wouldn't mind actually being friends with Naomi. Friends who occasionally fucked. Okay, friends who *frequently* fucked, because as much as he thought he'd enjoy hanging out and having real conversations with her, he couldn't deny he'd probably enjoy sleeping with her more.

In fact, he wouldn't mind meeting up for round three, if she was amenable.

Iain flipped through the contacts on his phone before he realized he didn't have her number. *Shit.* He could probably get it from Noah, but that might be weird. He didn't particularly care to explain how he'd left a business meeting without getting a potential contractor's phone number. He scratched his head and tried to figure out a way to get in touch with her. He supposed he could send her an email, but that assumed she'd see it and read it immediately. He had far too much excess energy to sit around waiting on that. Opening Google, he searched for NK Designs, hoping she had a website with a contact number listed. Bingo! Pressing his finger to the number, he brought the phone to his ear and listened to it ring on the other end.

After six long trills, her voicemail clicked on. *This is NK Designs. Leave a message after the tone, and I'll return your message within twenty-four hours.* It was obviously a business line, not her cell.

Iain jabbed the red 'end call' button and shoved his phone into his back pocket. He might not know how to get ahold of Naomi, but he couldn't sit in his room stewing any longer. Sure, he'd promised himself he would finish off his bottle of bourbon, but that wouldn't solve his problems any more than hanging up on his father would have. It might be too early to get drunk on booze, but there were no similar rules about sugar. Grabbing the keys to his rental off the small table located just inside his door, he spun them around his finger and made his way outside to the small blue Toyota he'd rented for the duration.

Ten minutes later he pulled up outside The Breadery, the bakery in the middle of River Hill known for both its bread and its pastries. Surveying the tarts and cakes on display in the front window for a couple of seconds, Iain pulled the door open. As the bell overhead chimed, he came to an immediate stop, a broad smile spreading across his lips. Sitting on a long wooden bench running along the side of the waiting area was a woman he knew tasted far better than any cake or cookie. And she looked good enough to eat.

9

"*H*eads up!"

Naomi looked up just in time to get hit in the face by a crinkled piece of parchment paper bearing The Breadery's logo. "If that had been my fritter, you would have been a dead man, Sean Amory," she called to the smirking blond man behind the counter.

"Worth it," he said. "Come and get it. Nice and toasty."

She levered herself off of the bench and got halfway to the counter before she realized who was standing just inside the door, smoldering at her. "Oh! Hi, Iain." She smiled at him, then crossed the rest of the distance to the counter to accept the wrapped package Sean was holding. She squinted up at the tall baker, lips tightening. His eyes were bleary, and the lines deepening across his jaw spoke of another long night down at the local dive bar. "Sean—"

He held up a hand. "Save it."

She scowled at him. "How long are you going to—"

"Oh, look, a customer," he said pointedly. "However can I help you, fine sir?"

Iain came up next to Naomi and perused the glass case. "What did you get?" he asked her.

She held up her treat. "Apple fritter. They only make them on Tuesdays." Because The Hut closed early on Monday nights, so Sean was sober enough to get up early to chop the apples. But that was neither here nor there. Iain didn't need to know about Noah's friend's sordid history or how he was coping with it any more than he needed to know about the little gathering Noah and Max were planning to figure out what to do about it. He wasn't a permanent fixture of their group, and he wasn't staying in River Hill.

"Sounds good to me." Iain turned back to Sean. "I'll have what she's having."

"How very *When Harry Met Sally*," Sean observed. Naomi shot him a warning glance, but he just laughed as he pulled another fritter out of the case and turned to put it into the heating oven on the back counter.

Iain shifted closer to Naomi, and she felt the warmth from his body seeping into her own. "How're you?" he asked.

"Fine."

"Sculpture coming along?"

She nodded. "The clay's finally dry enough to carve. It took a little longer than I expected, so I did some design work."

He winced. "Speaking of design work—"

She shook her head. "Iain ..."

"Naomi, I'm dying over here. I even talked to a couple of the people you recommended, and they're all giving me the same crap. Here, wait." He tugged his phone out of his pocket.

"Did you clearly and concisely explain what you needed?"

"Yes, I'm not an idiot. I've been in marketing for more than ten years." He tapped his phone's screen and then held it out to her. "This is all I can get out of anybody."

Naomi peered at the tiny image and wrinkled her nose. "Watercolor? Really?"

"It's on trend." He elongated the words, making them sound as pretentious as possible, and she laughed.

"I mean, it is, but it's the wrong approach for what you're doing, isn't it?"

He sighed. "Yes. And I can't get approval for the new label from my father anyway, so it probably doesn't matter."

Sean reappeared behind the counter and handed Iain his pastry. "Tough break, dude. Family businesses can be rough."

"You're familiar?"

Sean laughed, but to Naomi's ear, he didn't really sound all that amused "Oh, yes. The Breadery's been the Amory family business for generations. My mom owns it. I just work here."

Iain shook his head. "Got some new ideas you want to try out, do you?"

Sean's jaw tightened visibly. "Something like that. It's hard to argue with your family when they just want what's best for you, man."

Iain blew out another long breath. "Tell me about it. Sometimes I wonder whether they know me at all."

"That's true of families everywhere," Naomi said. "Business just makes it more complicated. When your livelihood is intertwined with your family, it's a lot harder to stand up and prove yourself."

"Were you ever in the family business?" Iain asked her.

"Please. Do these look like doctor's hands?" She held up the hand that wasn't clutching her fritter, showing off the streaks of clay and ink she hadn't bothered to scrub off.

Sean smirked at her. "Not cut out for it, huh?"

"Not interested. And don't poke fun at me, baker boy." She leveled a finger at him. "I'm leaving you alone. For now." Sean's drinking hadn't impacted anybody other than himself—yet—but it was only a matter of time. "Come on, Iain, let's leave him to wallow in his bread dough."

"Nice to meet you," Sean called as Iain held the door for her. "Hope you survive."

"Seems like a good guy," Iain remarked as he strolled down the street next to her. "Nice that he's on track to take over the family business, assuming that's what he wants to do."

She shook her head. "No way to tell. He used to be a record producer in L.A. Big time. Something happened and now he's back here." She paused. "He drinks a lot."

"I assume you don't mean that in the good way."

Iain made a living from selling alcohol, she realized. "Sorry. No." She winced. "Awkward."

He shrugged. "Appreciating it is different from drowning in it."

She nodded. "So, what are you going to do about your

problem, since we're not solving Sean's out here on the sidewalk?"

He grinned at her. "Actually, I'm pretty sure my problem can't be solved on the sidewalk either. At least, not if public decency laws are still a thing."

She laughed. "Oh, is that what we're talking about now?"

"Maybe." He unwrapped his fritter and took a bite. "This is really good."

"I know." She'd planned on taking hers straight home and devouring it while she stared at the clay and waited for inspiration to strike, but strolling along next to the sexy Irishman was unexpectedly fun. She folded the paper carefully down so she wouldn't get her fingers sticky and took her first bite. "So … your place or mine?"

He winced. "Given that 'my place' is still a tiny room at the Oakwell Inn, I'd be grateful to go to yours."

"Yeah? How grateful?"

*E*xtremely grateful, as it turned out. Naomi couldn't even regret the time lost working in her studio because yet again she jumped up out of bed crackling with creative energy.

She shook Iain, who was drowsing. "Do you mind if I go upstairs?"

"Mmph. Go for it." He scrubbed his hands over his eyes and stretched as she admired the play of his muscles. "Can I make some calls from your office?"

"Sure. It faces the front window and I don't have any

curtains, though. Fair warning." She grinned at him. "The neighbors might be curious."

He sat up, and her mouth watered a little at the sight of his bare chest. "Should I give them a show?" He flexed an arm.

"Depends on your goals." She laughed. "You might get a basket of brownies from Mr. Hughes, but Mr. Tidewell would probably critique your form."

"Aging bodybuilder?"

"Former Navy."

"Ouch. I'll put on a shirt, in the interest of international relations."

"I think we already had those," she teased as she headed out the bedroom door and up the stairs.

Two hours later, she sat up and stretched, sending a small avalanche of clay dust tumbling to the floor. "Damn. Every time."

"Art seems messy." Iain was at the door again.

"It is," she said ruefully. "There's a ShopVac in the closet."

"You ready for it? I can grab it." He moved toward the closet in the corner opposite the bathroom.

"Sure. I need a break." She'd finally gotten the curve of the biggest element shaped the way she wanted, but how to pull off the next part still eluded her.

He rummaged in the closet for a bit and then pulled the large, wheeled vacuum out. "Got a plug?"

"Right there." She pointed.

He rolled the vacuum to her, then unwound the cord and plugged it in. "Here you go."

"Thanks." She made quick work of vacuuming up the

piles of dust, then ran the hose over her shirt a couple of times. "Done."

"That how you do laundry?"

"What, they do it differently in Ireland?"

He laughed. "Talk about cultural differences."

She unplugged the vacuum and put it away, then shooed him out of the studio and down the stairs.

"So, do you know what you're making yet?" He followed her into the bedroom as she stripped off the dusty shirt and dropped it into her laundry basket.

"Sort of." It wasn't what she'd expected it to be, but if she could get the clay to reveal what she saw in her mind, it would be some of her best work. She went into the bathroom to brush additional dust out of her hair.

"I just don't get how you see what's inside the clay," Iain said thoughtfully. He was perched on the edge of her bed, watching her through the open bathroom door.

She twisted her hair into a quick ponytail and shrugged. "Years of practice? Innate talent? Artistic genius? How do you know what a new whiskey is going to taste like?"

He looked at her and smirked. "I taste it."

"Oh. Maybe that was the wrong metaphor."

He laughed as she pulled a fresh tank top out of her dresser. "I get where you were going with it, though."

"Did you get all your calls made?" she asked, gesturing for him to lead the way toward her home office.

"Most of them. I stole some of your printer paper to take notes." He picked up a folded sheaf of paper and waved it at her. His handwriting was neat, she noticed. Lots of slashing angles, but very readable.

"There's plenty of notepads," she said mildly.

"Yes, but I didn't want to disturb your sketches. Particularly not this one." He held up the notepad closest to her computer and she winced. "Want to talk about it?"

"No."

"Naomi, this is the perfect logo for my whiskey. I thought you weren't working on it."

"I'm not."

He shook the paper at her like she was a puppy who'd done something naughty. "Then what is this?"

"I just jotted it down while I was thinking about something else."

"Can I pay you for it?"

She reached out and snatched the notepad out of his grasp. "No. It's proprietary."

"Which means what?"

"Which means you're not taking my sketch and getting some hack to brand it up for you."

"Then why won't you do it?"

"Because I don't work for people I'm sleeping with. It's bad business." She tore off the top sheet and folded it carefully.

He sighed. "Fine. I'm too hungry to argue about it. Want to go out to dinner?"

She opened her mouth to say yes, then froze. What was she doing? Spending the entire day with him? Hanging out at home, working side-by-side, having dinner together? This was starting to feel like a relationship. And Naomi didn't *do* relationships.

Relationships turned men into bizarre, greedy animals who demanded that you give up all of your time and energy for them. Just look at her parents and her brother and his wife. Both her mother and her sister-in-law had completely subsumed their own lives into their husbands'. Now, they spent all of their time supporting the ambitions of the men in their lives, with nothing of their own to show for it. Like hell was Naomi going to turn into some kind of Stepford Wife.

"I can't," she said. "Sorry."

He frowned. "But—"

"You should probably go," she added quickly. "I've got a lot of work to do, and you probably have some more calls and meetings."

"Actually—"

"I'll see you around." She pasted on a smile and led the way to the door before he could get a word in edgewise. "Here you go." She opened the door and held a hand out like she was a game show hostess demonstrating a prize.

"Er… thanks." He stepped over the threshold, then turned back to her. "Naomi, I—"

"Bye!" She shut the door in his face. Then she leaned against it and put her hand to her forehead. *What a narrow escape.*

10

———

"There is nothing out there." Iain groaned and shoved a taco into his mouth, savoring the succulent pork. Max was testing out a new recipe. As far as Iain was concerned, his new friend had outdone himself.

Noah set a bucket of beer on the table, and Angelica grabbed one of the bottles and twisted the top off. "How much are you looking to spend?" Noah asked, settling in next to his girlfriend on the leather bench.

Iain wiped his mouth. "I'm looking to keep it under two thousand a month, but I'm starting to think that's not enough."

Angelica took a long drink. "No wonder you can't find a place. That's chump change around here, Iain."

"It's not the money, not really. It's mostly that I can't commit to signing a long lease. And every landlord I've talked to wants first and last month's rent. Meanwhile, that's literally all I need. I might have to stay at Oakwell after all."

"You still looking for a place to stay?" Max asked, setting down a plate of pickled radishes and jalapeños and sliding into the booth next to him.

Iain nodded and spun his beer bottle within the ring of condensation that had accumulated on the table in front of him. "It's brutal out there, man."

"The people who owned my place before me put in a studio apartment above the garage. It's got a dorm fridge and hot plate, so the kitchen's pretty much worthless, but it's yours if you want it, however long you need it. You can pay me whatever you feel is fair."

That was the best news he'd heard all day. Not that it was too hard to earn that distinction—from the time he'd woken up, his day had been filled with one bit of bad news after the next. Before he'd made his way down to Frankie's, a graphic artist he'd been about to hire had let him know she could no longer work with him since she'd just taken a contract with another distiller. Personally, Iain didn't consider them competition—they made flavored vodkas, of all things—but their head of marketing definitely considered anyone with the last name of Brennan *his* competition, so now Iain was back to square one on that front too. If Max was willing to let him crash above his garage for the next two months, he'd take it.

"Are you sure?"

"Yeah, of course. I only put my gym equipment up there because I felt like the space was going to waste and I felt guilty." Max shrugged. "Which reminds me—if you're going to move in, I'll need your help moving my gym equipment into the garage. And it could probably use a deep clean." He scratched his chin. "And some towels and bed linens. Pretty much everything, to be honest."

Angelica bounced in her seat and clapped her hands. "Ooh, can I help?"

Noah barked out an emphatic "No," while at the same time Iain exclaimed "Yes!"

Noah shot him an exasperated look. "Dude, no. She's only home for four weeks before she starts filming again in fuck knows where, and I intend to keep her busy for all of them."

Angelica bumped Noah's shoulder with her own. "It's Portland. And you're a pig."

"That's not what you said last night." Noah waggled his eyebrows, before inhaling the rest of his taco in one bite.

She rolled her eyes and slapped her palms down onto the wooden tabletop. "Anyhow …" she said pointedly, "I would love to help. I was planning to do a Tar-jay run on Friday morning. Need to refill a few essentials for the inn."

"Tar-jay?"

"Sorry, I mean Target—only the best, most amazing store in all of Christendom. My personal philosophy is if you can't find it there, it doesn't exist." Her eyes took on a dreamy cast.

"Sounds expensive." Iain wasn't cheap, but he didn't think forking over a ton of cash to kit out a temporary home was the wisest decision. He'd already spent way too much staying at Angelica's bed and breakfast, though it had been nice having daily maid service.

"That's the great thing about Target. It's not expensive—"

"Says the woman who regularly spends two hundred dollars when she goes there for 'just one thing.'" Noah raised a sardonic eyebrow at her.

Angelica chuckled. "Guilty as charged. That's the *downside* of Target—you go in with a small list, but then walk out with an overflowing cart full of stuff you never even knew you wanted."

While that might be true for Angelica, Iain doubted he'd suffer the same problem since he'd never had any difficulty before sticking to a to-do list … or a budget. Quickly, he went over his schedule for the week. He had a couple of meetings with restaurant owners in Napa on Monday, and Oakland and Berkeley on Tuesday. And apparently he'd need to help Max move his gym equipment downstairs by Wednesday, so he could hopefully get a cleaner in on Thursday. As it turned out, Friday worked perfectly. "Okay, count me in."

"Traitor," Noah whispered, downing the remainder of his beer.

"Knock, knock." Angelica popped her head through Iain's open doorway. "You ready, Freddie?"

"Yup." He slid his phone into the front pocket of his jeans and palmed his keys on the way out. "I'm warning you though. I hate shopping."

Angelica gave him a quick once over as they walked down a manicured path toward the gravel-lined parking lot at the side of the inn. "I figured as much."

"What's that supposed to mean?" he asked, climbing into the passenger seat of her BMW.

"You've been here a month, and I've seen you wear two things—a black suit and this ensemble." She flicked her fingers toward him, then started the engine of her car.

Iain glanced down. "What's wrong with what I'm wearing?" He had on black boots, black jeans, a gray thermal henley, and a black leather jacket. His nods to accessorizing were a black and gray herringbone pattern flat cap, a black scarf, and his watch. He thought he looked damn good, even if he did say so himself. His look was spartan, but it worked for him. He was a bit miffed Angelica didn't appreciate it.

"Not a thing." She looked both ways and then pulled out into traffic. "But you have to admit, it's not very creative."

"No, it's not," he agreed with a chuckle. He didn't have time to say anything more in defense of his clothes, because she reached out, turned the volume up on the radio, and began singing along with the lyrics at the top of her lungs. The songs were familiar, and her good mood was unmistakable. Now and then, she'd toss him a happy, carefree look. It was so infectious that by the time they turned off the highway and into the suburban shopping center, he was singing too. No wonder Noah was captivated.

"I give you Mecca," she said with mock reverence as she pulled her car into a parking spot and then jumped out to wave grandiosely at the red-topped building in front of them.

Iain unfastened the belt at his thigh and slid out of his

seat, taking a quick glance around. With no small amount of horror, he realized there were maybe four hundred other cars in the parking lot with them. A complete disinterest in fashion wasn't the only thing that usually kept him from shopping trips. He wondered if he could bribe Angelica to shop for him while he waited in the car and caught up on his email on his phone.

Apparently, he'd inadvertently telegraphed his intent.

Angelica took one look at him and shook her head. Looping her arm through his, she tugged him forward. "Oh, no, you don't. You're coming with me, mister."

Half an hour later, he could *almost* admit he'd been hasty in wanting to skip out on the shopping trip when they'd first arrived. That was, until a kid still wearing his bed clothes came tearing around a corner screaming something about Transformers, his frazzled mom chasing after him with an infant strapped to her front. Iain shuddered as he watched her take off down an aisle calling after her wayward son.

"Not a fan of kids?" Angelica asked, wheeling her nearly-full cart alongside his mostly empty one.

Iain debated how best to answer. It was his experience that women of a certain age had a tendency to be mad for babies, and when they encountered a man who wasn't, they tried their damnedest to convince him otherwise. Even his sister—the most logical and reasonable woman he knew … not to mention entirely single and nowhere near having kids herself—had accused him of being full of shit when he'd told her he didn't see himself settling down and starting a family anytime soon. If ever.

"Kids are grand, but …"

"But you don't want any of your own." It wasn't a question so much as a statement of fact.

"I'm still on the fence about it." Although he was leaning pretty strongly toward the 'nope' side.

Angelica nodded. "I always just assumed I'd have a family one day, but 'one day' always seemed like it was in the far-off future. And then I met Noah, and he wants like a whole fucking gaggle of them, so …" She looked back over her shoulder toward where the woman and her kids had disappeared. "But I'm pretty sure I won't be bringing any of them with me to Target. This is my sacred space."

Iain laughed and added a box of instant noodles to his cart. He wouldn't ever admit it out loud, but he was quickly coming to love Target nearly as much as Angelica did. He also wouldn't say aloud how much he liked her. She was forthright and refreshing, and she didn't take herself too seriously. In fact, the whole group of friends he'd somehow stumbled into in River Hill all seemed to be generally laid back and easy going. They were a far cry from the boisterous friends he'd left back in Ireland. Hanging out with them these last few weeks had made his time in California more enjoyable than it would have been otherwise.

Them, and a particular female sculptor he hadn't heard from in a handful of days.

After the odd way Naomi had booted him out of her house, he'd backed off and given her space. He thought they'd had a really great afternoon together, but now he wondered if maybe he'd misread the signals. The sex had been fantastic—again—but she'd still sent him packing. Iain liked Naomi—probably more than he should—but he wasn't going to beg her to like him back. If she wanted nothing to do with him, so be it.

Except …

"I was wondering—" he stopped his cart in front of a display of brightly-colored towels and studied them more attentively than they deserved "—do you know Noah's friend Naomi Klein?"

Angelica stopped next to him, and when she turned to face him, he was startled to find her easy-going charm had been replaced by a sharp-edged intensity. "Why? What have you heard?"

Shit. That wasn't good. Maybe there was some bad blood between the two women he wasn't aware of. But if so, why would Noah have recommended Naomi to him in the first place? He could be surly at times, but the man wasn't blind or stupid. And he very obviously loved Angelica. Disgustingly so, Iain sometimes thought. And yet, her sharp response just now suggested there was definitely something there.

"I'm sorry. Forget I asked."

"No, I want to know. What have people been telling you?"

Wait, what? "Nothing, I swear. I was looking for a graphic designer when I first got here and Noah introduced us. She and I …" He tunneled his hand through his hair and slid it to the back of his neck, which he could feel growing damp with discomfort. He wasn't one to kiss-and-tell, but he felt like he had to say *something* since Angelica had obviously gotten the wrong idea. "I like her, but she runs hot and cold, and I was just wondering if you had any insight into why." He shook his head and took a step back, his hands held out in front of him, palms out. "But like I said, forget I asked."

Angelica let out a deep sigh. "Sorry for the overreaction. It's just that River Hill is a small town, with some small-minded people. Some who enjoy reminding me that Noah and Naomi have known each other a really long time. And I get *really* tired of them trying to tell everyone else about it, too. Like, we *know*."

Iain let out his own sigh of relief and felt his shoulders relaxing. He'd been worried there for a second. "He mentioned something about that when he gave me her card, which is why I figured I could ask your advice."

Angelica's brows drew down. "When I say they've 'known each other,' I mean in the biblical sense … if you get my drift." She rolled her eyes. "Their parents thought they'd get married someday."

"Oh."

"Yeah, oh."

"Fuck. I'm sorry I asked. Let's pretend I didn't."

She shook her head, but her eyes remained guarded. "No, it's okay. The thing is, I adore Naomi. She's nice and funny, and she doesn't take shit from anyone. I can appreciate that about her. She and Noah *are* really great friends, and I'm definitely not the kind of woman who tells her boyfriend he has to stop talking to someone who's been in his life forever just because they used to have sex. I mean, I don't love that she knows what his dick looks like, and I get tired of *hearing* about it from other people, but I *trust* him. And I trust her too, if that makes any difference in what you were going to ask."

"That's very …" He trailed off, at a loss for words. He

couldn't imagine how he'd react if put in a similar situation. Although, he kind of was now, wasn't he? He wasn't a permanent fixture in River Hill like Angelica was, but he *did* consider Noah a friend. Hearing that his friend and the woman he wanted to spend the next two months with had once been fuck buddies … well, he wasn't particularly thrilled.

From the beginning, he'd known Naomi didn't view sex the way most women he knew did. And Angelica was right—Naomi didn't take shit from anyone. He liked that about her. In truth, he liked *so* many things about her.

But now he wondered if this new-found knowledge would be at the back of his mind the next time they were together. Assuming, of course, there was a next time. Going by recent events, he wasn't really sure.

Angelica laid a hand on his bicep. "I won't pry, but I will say this: Naomi is a really good person, and I consider her a friend. But she's also super gun-shy about relationships. Noah's told me about it, and she has, too. If you're serious about her, you should probably go in with your eyes wide open. She's not the type of person who makes promises of forever."

Iain swallowed. That should have been music to his ears, but it wasn't. For some strange reason, Angelica's words settled in the pit of his belly like sludge. He didn't understand why, so he pushed that feeling aside. "If that's the case, it's probably good that I'll be gone in two months, then."

She pulled her hand away and peered at him, one eyebrow raised in speculation. Eventually, she nodded once. "Yeah, it probably is."

11

———

"Stop fidgeting, Naomi." Her mother's commanding tone made Naomi realize she'd been tugging at the hem of her dress.

"Sorry." She clasped her hands together in front of her like a child in a school picture.

"Don't do that either, it makes your bosom cave in."

"Thanks, Mom." She sighed.

"You're not here to mope, darling. You're here to be charming and remind the Board that they're lucky to have a man as talented as your father as a candidate."

"How could I possibly remind them any more than you're already doing?"

"By standing there and being single," her mother said sweetly.

Tanya, standing next to Naomi, choked on her champagne as she stifled a laugh.

Naomi gave her sister-in-law her best evil eye. "You want to say something?"

"I wouldn't dare." Tanya grinned at her. "I'm perfectly happy back here, out of the spotlight."

"Nice try," Naomi muttered, then raised her voice. "Mom, don't you think Tanya's boobs look great in that dress?"

Her mother's eagle eye fastened on Tanya's impressive cleavage. "Tanya, go talk to Dr. Mutternauer. He loves busty, unavailable blondes."

Tanya rolled her eyes. "That's me."

"I'm going to make you a t-shirt that says Busty Unavailable Blonde," Naomi said.

"Oh, good, I'll wear it to the kids' soccer games." With that, Tanya headed off to her target, an undecided Board member.

Naomi would be glad when the hospital Board made their decision. The meeting to decide who would be the next Chief of Medicine at San Francisco General was in a few weeks, and as it got closer, her parents were getting more frenetic in their attempts to seal the deal for her father. Hence her presence here, at yet another charity gala. This one benefitted the city's food bank, so she could hardly begrudge it, but she was definitely more weary of the parade of social events this year than she usually was.

She loved her family dearly but had never managed quite the same amount of separation as Noah had from his. But then, his dream career fell right in line with what his family thought he ought to be doing. They'd just wanted him to do it for them, not himself. Naomi's family didn't think art was a real job. And if she wasn't going to *be* a doctor or a lawyer, they would prefer she marry one.

She suppressed a shudder. Marriage was the *last* thing

she wanted to think about. Especially here. Right on cue, her mother tapped her shoulder. "Naomi. Avi Hershfeld is here."

"So?"

"So, you should talk to him."

"You forced me to go on a date with Avi when I was sixteen. He groped me in the back of the car and then told me I should get implants like his sister."

"He's a very successful entertainment lawyer now."

"That doesn't surprise me at *all*."

"Well, what about—"

Naomi turned to her mother, surprised by the sudden rage that was boiling in her belly. She'd been listening to the litany of available men in her parents' circles for years. Why it was making her so angry today, she had no idea. "I'm *not interested.* I'm here to help Dad. I'm *happy* to help Dad. I want him to get what he wants. But why can't you be interested in what *I* want?"

Her mother blinked. "What do you want?"

Naomi sighed. "Did you know that I just signed a lucrative contract with Z Gallery?"

"Good for you, dear. What does that have to do with your relationship status?"

"Nothing."

"Well, then." Her mother heaved a small, satisfied sigh as though she'd won the argument. "When you find the right man, Naomi, you'll know."

Naomi rolled her eyes. The hurt she felt whenever her mother showed she thought marriage was the only thing good enough for her daughter was an old, familiar ache. But she wasn't going to resolve it here, in the middle of a crowded ballroom. She was pretty sure therapists didn't make house calls, let alone gala calls.

Although there probably *were* some pretty good psychologists in the crowd tonight. She eyed the people around her, wondering if she could trick somebody into convincing her mother to attend therapy.

"Naomi."

"Hmm?"

"I'm speaking to you, dear."

"Sorry. What?"

"Can you ask your father what the name of that whiskey he liked at dinner last night was? I want to pick some up for his office."

"Brennan's," Naomi said without thinking. Her mother's sudden silence made her realize what she'd just said. Naomi never—*never*—knew random trivia about her father's alcohol preferences. She looked over at her mother, who was looking back at her with a raised eyebrow. "I mean, I think it was Brennan's. I'll, um, go ask him."

The very last thing she needed was her mother learning anything about Iain Brennan. The woman was a fiend with Google. Plus, Naomi had shut the door in Iain's face and barely spoken to him for days. He was probably on his way out of town right about now.

Her phone buzzed as she escaped from her mother's orbit. She glanced down at the notification to see a text from Angelica. She grinned. Noah's girlfriend was swiftly becoming a good friend, and she was glad. Thank goodness it hadn't gotten awkward between them. The content of the text wiped the smile straight off of her face.

Angelica had taken Iain shopping? To outfit the apartment above Max's *garage*? What was happening? Was the man relocating to River Hill? She thought he had two months to get his sales deals in order for the new line of whiskey. She'd assumed that meant he'd be traveling up and down the coast, hustling. Or whatever one did to sell whiskey. Avoiding him was going to be a lot harder if he was staying around for another sixty days. On the other hand … he was only here for two more months. That was what he'd said, specifically. Then it was back to Ireland. Two months of fantastic sex sounded pretty damn nice.

She flipped her phone over against her palm, running her thumb along the smooth case thoughtfully. Her last piece for Z Gallery was due in a similar timeframe. She'd need to supervise the installation and attend the opening. An easy out if he got clingy when it came time to part. Naomi let her lips curve into a smile. Maybe she could have her cake, and sleep with it, too.

"Miss Naomi!" A familiar voice broke into her musing, and she turned with the smile still on her face.

"Hi, Luis. I didn't realize you'd be here." She pursed her lips. "How silly of me. Of course you are."

Luis Montero was one of her father's best friends. He was perilously close to being a celebrity chef, as his restaurants won as much acclaim as his high-profile relationships. She'd always adored him, and secretly wondered why such an interesting man seemed to have such a genuine friendship with her extremely boring father. When she'd been in her late twenties, Luis had finally let her in on some of the more hair-raising exploits the two of them had shared before Naomi and Jacob had been born. The friendship made a little more sense now, but she still couldn't picture her father doing any of the things Luis had described. Or her mother, for that matter.

She hugged the older man, then let him grasp her arms and kiss her cheek before pushing her back to look her over. "You have opinions?"

"You're a credit to your family," Luis said.

"Great. Just what I've always wanted to be."

He laughed. "I saw something about Z Gallery. Big time stuff, Miss Naomi."

"Thanks. I'm pretty excited about it."

"You going to make something for my next restaurant?"

"I don't know. Are you going to pay me for it?" she teased. He'd given her one of her first big breaks, displaying several pieces she'd created during her Tuscan phase in one of his popular restaurants. Sure, she wanted to make it on her own artistic talents, but she wasn't opposed to a bit of nepotism when it benefited her career. Plus, she'd given them to him for free, and when the restaurant had closed a few years ago, he'd sold them for a tidy profit, something she was fairly sure he wasn't aware she knew.

"We'll work something out," he said.

"What kind of restaurant are you opening next?" It seemed like Luis was always opening something. His restaurants were always successful, and he didn't stick to one type of cuisine, something she appreciated.

"My girlfriend calls it hipster comfort food." His latest girlfriend was an actress on a TV crime drama. Naomi hadn't met her, but Luis tended to have relatively good taste in women. Nearly all of his exes were still friends with him. If she were interested in having relationships, she might have asked how he managed it. Two months enthusiastically fucking Iain Brennan wouldn't count as a relationship, would it? *Nah.*

"We've got the design and most of the initial menu worked out," Luis was saying. "Working on vendor agreements now. Gotta get the very best behind the bar and in our kitchen, you know? I'm trying to find all new stuff for this one, introduce people to tastes they haven't had before."

Vendor agreements. Naomi opened her mouth, then closed it. Iain's new whiskey was probably the sort of thing Luis was looking for. One word from her, and Iain would have a contract with one of the biggest restaurant owners in California. She could use her connections to help him. Just like her mother would for her father.

Something uncomfortable squirmed in the base of her stomach, and she felt herself going cold. If she put in a good word for Iain right now, it could be a huge break for his career. But it would turn her into The Supportive Girlfriend. She wasn't his girlfriend. She wanted him to do well in his chosen field, and she certainly hoped that his new brand succeeded. But using her social connections to make it happen for him?

The idea made her faintly nauseous. It was the same feeling she got every time she stood at the door of her parents' penthouse, waiting for her mother to open it and ask why she wasn't married yet, or if she'd met the son of one of the members of the hospital's Board yet.

"I hope it goes well," she blurted. "I'm sorry, Luis, I'm supposed to be asking my dad something."

She fled, leaving Luis alone. He'd cope. She, on the other hand, was in desperate need of some time to think. She found a bathroom and locked herself in, leaning against the door and closing her eyes.

Why was nepotism fine for her own career, but bad when it came to helping Iain? She rubbed her forehead and wondered if she ought to see if any of the fancy psychologists hobnobbing in the crowd wanted to give her a freebie in the back hallway. She clearly had some issues to work out.

And now, faint guilt was starting to overtake her. Sure, she'd been sleeping with Iain, and had extensive and fairly lurid plans to continue doing so, but he was also a perfectly nice guy. Noah, Max, Angelica, and her other friends all seemed to like him a lot, too. She could have done him the favor as a friend. Couldn't she?

Except asking for this particular favor in this specific crowd didn't come off as friendship. It brought her dangerously close to Stepford territory. And she wasn't going there. Ever.

She sighed. She couldn't handle helping Iain the way her mother would expect her to. A flicker of the white towels folded neatly on the counter by the sinks caught her eye. For some reason, her mind went back to her office, and the logo she'd sketched while she'd been pondering Max's menus.

Sometimes, when she was working out a design plan, she let her fingers draw whatever they felt like. It was the closest using pen and ink ever felt to working with clay, leaving herself at the mercy of whatever creative breeze the universe felt like throwing her way. That day, what had blown in was a logo for Whitman's Revival, the W forming bold strokes accented by curving serifs that led into the dots of holly-like berries and quickly-drawn tiny sparkles and leaf shapes. It really was the perfect logo, evoking the nostalgia of handmade with some of the flavors that Iain had described to her.

Maybe she could help him in a different way. She couldn't bring herself to talk to Luis for Iain, but she could take the branding job he'd been trying to hire her for since he'd arrived in River Hill. Helping him with her *actual* skills was a far cry from begging her friends and family to play nice. Iain was a good marketer, a great salesman. With the right branding package, he'd meet his quota without even trying. And then she could sleep easy. Or not sleep, if her two-months-of-hot-sex plan worked out the way she was hoping.

She pulled her phone out and fired off a text to Iain before she could rethink it. *I'll do your logo.*

12

———

"Thank you for doing this," Iain said, the pad of his index finger tracing over the design Naomi had created for Whitman's Revival. "To be honest, I wasn't sure I'd hear from you again. You kind of ghosted me." They were in her kitchen once again, this time sitting across from each other at her table discussing the logo and branding package he'd just signed a contract to hire her to develop. Finally.

He glanced up in time to catch her looking away guiltily. "Yeah, about that—"

"I'm not asking you to explain yourself. I get it. We had some fun, and now it's time to move on."

Naomi's eyes came back around, the guilt replaced with what Iain thought looked a whole lot like contemplation. "Funny you should mention that."

"Funny how?"

"I was thinking," she said, her finger swirling a pattern on the table that separated them. "You're leaving in two months, and it would be a shame if we didn't spend that time ... hanging out." Her eyes bored into his, as if daring him to misunderstand what she was inferring.

His lips quirked up into a smirk. "Why, Miss Klein, are you asking me to fuck you senseless until I board a plane back to Ireland?"

She tossed him a wicked smile full of promise. "You have to admit; we're pretty damn good at it."

"The best," he agreed. He felt his chest sawing in and out as his breathing became deeper and more labored. Iain couldn't remember the last time he'd felt such heady anticipation. Oh, wait, yes, he could. It was that night in San Francisco when he and Naomi had practically run from that dive bar to his hotel. He'd been so ready for her that he'd ripped her dress off before the door to his room had locked behind them.

"So, what do you say, Brennan? You want to spend the next sixty days seeing how many orgasms we can give each other?"

That was all the invitation Iain needed. Abruptly, he stood, his chair scraping over the black-and-white-checked linoleum and then crashing to the floor. He stalked around the fifties-style diner table and fisted his hands in Naomi's hair. He bent at the waist and let his lips hover scant centimeters from her parted ones. He could feel the warmth of her breath mingling with his own. "What do you say we get started on that now?"

She licked her lips. "Yes, let's."

Permission granted, Iain's mouth crashed down onto Naomi's with a fierceness he hadn't anticipated. He knew he'd been craving another taste of her, but he hadn't realized just how much until their tongues twisted and slid together. He groaned and took their kiss deeper. Naomi wrapped her arms around his neck and tugged him closer, as if she wanted to climb him like the oak tree in her front garden.

They broke apart, and Iain sucked in a lungful of air. "Bedroom. Now."

She hopped up onto the table and shook her head. Reaching for his belt buckle, she said, "Kitchen. Now."

"So demanding," he chuckled, letting her fingers work their magic. When she wrapped them around his cock and stroked upward, her thumb coasting over his crown, he hissed, and his head fell back with a moan. God, this woman knew exactly how to get him going.

Naomi wrapped her long, lithe leg around his hip and tugged him forward. "I want you inside me."

All at once, realization hit, and Iain paused his forward momentum. Flattening his palms on either side of Naomi, he groaned—and not the kind that usually preceded having sex. "Shit, I don't have a condom." They'd used the one he carried in his wallet the last time he'd been here, and when she'd kicked him out afterward, he hadn't gotten around to replacing it. Hadn't seen the point, really.

Naomi studied him intently for a few charged beats. "I don't have any either. But I have an IUD, and I get tested three times a year whether I need to or not. I'm clean."

So was he, but ... damn.

Naomi's words—*her offer*—rattled around inside his head. The only time he'd ever gone without protection was his first time. After which he'd spent two solid weeks convinced life as he knew it was over. It wasn't until his girlfriend—who'd also been a virgin—had told him she'd had her period that Iain had been able to breathe again. He'd promised himself he'd never put himself through that again.

But this was different. Wasn't it?

He and Naomi weren't two awkward teenagers fumbling around in the dark while their parents had dinner upstairs, and he certainly wasn't a two-pump chump anymore either. That had been the worst part of that whole ordeal; he hadn't meant to come in Mary. He'd thought he had plenty of time to pull out once he'd gotten her off. That was the Catholic way, after all. Unfortunately, things hadn't quite gone according to plan, and he'd been wrapping it up ever since.

Could he do this? He trusted Naomi. And that was the craziest part of all. He did, absolutely. He hadn't known her long, but he knew deep in his gut that she wasn't lying just to get him to fuck her. Back home, that wasn't always the case. His name—and the sizable fortune that went with it—was a hell of a motivator for a particular kind of person. Ones he usually tried to stay far, far away from.

"Never mind," Naomi said, breaking into his thoughts. "Forget I said anything." She looked embarrassed by his silence, and Iain realized she must have taken it as rejection. She dropped her leg and tried to slide away.

"Don't move; I'm thinking."

She sighed. "Iain, if you have to think that long about whether or not you want to go bare, it's not the right decision. Don't worry about it. It was a dumb idea anyway." Pasting a fake smile on her face—he'd seen her real one, and this wasn't it—she tried to lighten the mood.

"Let's go in the living room. There are plenty of ways to get each other off without having sex." She waggled her eyebrows, and he almost believed the act.

But the thing was, he didn't want her going down on him. Okay, sure. He'd *love* that—some other time. Right now, he wanted to make *her* feel good, and hopefully recapture some of the spark they'd lost.

"I like you here just fine." He nuzzled the spot just behind her ear that he knew turned her on.

She let out a contented sigh, but her body remained tense.

Time to turn things up a notch, Brennan.

"On second thought," he said, tugging her forward until her ass was almost off the table, "I like you better *here*." He dropped to his knees between Naomi's spread legs and raised his gaze to meet hers.

"Iain?"

That wasn't a no … but it wasn't a yes either.

"Let me. Please." He set his palms on her thighs and coasted upward, until her skirt bunched around her waist. "Yes?"

Naomi chewed her lip, and he held his breath waiting for her decision. After a few seconds, she nodded and flashed him a real smile. "Yes, you fiend."

Returning that smile with a wicked grin of his own, Iain set to work driving her crazy.

Drawing the cotton panel of her underwear aside, he bent forward, pulling her sweet, spicy scent into his nose. He teased her with light flicks of his tongue, and she wiggled as if to move away, but he held her still. Finally, when she began making desperate little noises low in the back of her throat, Iain set his lips to her petal-soft skin.

She tangled her fingers in his hair, and for a brief moment, he worried she might put a stop to his eager explorations. Eager to finish what he'd started, he flattened his tongue and licked a broad path over her seam. And then, with a long, anguished moan, Naomi pulled him tight against her, and Iain set to work making her come apart.

"Here you go." Naomi set a grilled cheese sandwich down in front of Iain before dropping into the seat across from him with one of her own. "It's not Frankie's, but you won't starve either."

Iain bit into the toasty bread and melted cheese concoction and stifled an appreciative moan. Swallowing, he said, "You won't hear me complain when a beautiful woman decides to feed me." He took another big bite, letting her see how much he enjoyed this. It wasn't just the food either, although that was good too. It was hanging out, getting to know each other better. It was not being kicked to the curb two seconds after having one of the most intense orgasms of his life. If ever there was a way to kill one's post-coital high, it was immediately being shown to the door.

"At the risk of sounding too couple-y," Naomi drawled, "how was your day?" Her face looked pained, almost as if it cost her something dear to ask him such a basic question.

He chuckled and shook his head. "Asking me about my job doesn't make you my girlfriend, Naomi."

She grabbed her bottle of beer and tipped her head back as she swallowed. Iain tried not to get too distracted by the sight of her throat working. He blinked and shook his head to push those dirty fantasies aside.

"No, it doesn't," she agreed. "But letting you give me orgasms and then asking about your day? That comes dangerously close." She raised an eyebrow, as if daring him to contradict the sentiment.

To avoid having to offer up an immediate opinion, Iain stuffed his mouth full of the remainder of his meal and spent longer than necessary chewing. It was a good thing Angelica had given him a heads up about Naomi's fear of commitment. Not that he wasn't intimately familiar with it already, but at least now he knew it wasn't an issue with him specifically.

Not that you're looking for a girlfriend, he reminded himself.

And yet, he didn't relish the idea of them being completely casual either. It would be easy to spend the next two months fucking Naomi whenever they each had an itch that needed scratching, but that just wasn't him. He hadn't been in a serious relationship in a long time, but the women he'd slept with between then and now fell into one of two categories: either they were of the one-and-done variety—like when he was traveling—or he remained friendly with them. Sometimes they were both, to be honest. Maybe it made him old-fashioned, but if a woman was good enough for him to stick his dick in, she was more than good enough to have a conversation with.

And he very much enjoyed conversations with this particular one. He wasn't going to force Naomi to be friends, but he was going to let her know this wasn't just about sex for him. If it turned out that's all she wanted from him, the next sixty days were going to be … hard.

"Tell me if you think I've got it wrong," Iain pushed his plate away and sat back in his chair, "but we get along pretty well."

Naomi sat back too, mimicking his posture. "Yes?" The word came out sounding more like a question than an answer; like she wasn't sure where he was going with this line of questioning, and she didn't want to commit to something she might have to walk back later.

Iain chuckled and shook his head. If he wasn't so fecking charmed by her, he might be exasperated instead. Miss Naomi Klein really was the biggest commitment-phobe he'd ever met—and that was saying something. Undeterred, he pressed on. "And this is nice."

She nodded slowly, and her pulse visibly kicked in her neck. "It is."

"And it might be fun if, in addition to giving each other epic orgasms, we also hung out sometimes. Not as my girlfriend—" he rushed to clarify "—but as my *friend*. A friend I think is beautiful, funny, smart, and talented. A friend I like talking to *and* fucking."

She stared at him for a beat and then swallowed deeply. "We could do that."

Suddenly, Iain felt guilty. Not guilty enough to take it all back, mind you, but enough to want to set her worried mind at ease. He leaned forward and squeezed her fingers. "Relax, Naomi. I just want to hang out with you while I'm here. I'm not asking you to marry me. Sixty days … that's all. After that, I'll be gone. And then years from now you can sit around with your girlfriends, drinking a bottle of Noah's wine, gossiping about the sexy Irishman who made you come like no one ever had before. Or since." He winked and slid his hand away, watching as her shoulders instantly relaxed. Good; now he was getting somewhere.

Almost as if a switch had been flipped, Naomi's face came alive and her eyes danced. "I think I like the way you think, Iain Brennan."

13

$\mathcal{A}$ week later, Naomi pushed her empty plate away. "That was delicious."

Angelica beamed at her. "I'm so glad you liked it."

"I had no idea you cooked." Angelica had spent years as a popular character actress, an occupation that hadn't left her much time for eating, let alone cooking, as far as Naomi knew.

"Max has been giving her lessons," Noah said over the rim of his wine glass.

"Oh, boo, he told you." Angelica frowned. "I was hoping you thought I was some kind of savant."

Noah laughed. "I love you, and you're brilliant in many ways, but going straight from grilled cheese to beef bourguignon was a stretch for believability."

Naomi watched their interplay fondly. They really were good for each other. Noah had been on the verge of serious Grumpy Old Man-hood before Angelica had moved in next door to him. They'd battled each other on many fronts before figuring out their heated exchanges were actually sparked by a major attraction. And then Noah had done what nobody had expected him to: decided Angelica was worth putting aside all of his weird family issues and making a real commitment.

So now here they all were, having dinner in Noah's modern kitchen. He'd asked for Naomi's help in convincing Angelica to take the next step and actually marry him. Why he thought Naomi would be a good choice as advocate, she had no idea. She was probably the least marriage-minded person he knew. Presumably, even Max and Sean wanted to get married someday, while she had no interest whatsoever in the institution. But she had known Noah since they were children, so apparently she was his first line of attack.

"So, Angelica, what's your schedule like coming up?" She tried to keep it casual. Not that it mattered. Angelica was no dummy. She probably knew perfectly well what Noah's plans were. How she would respond was a mystery to everyone but her—something that drove Noah crazy. Naomi appreciated that.

"We're shooting for three weeks in Portland, and then we have to double back to do a few re-shoots in Colorado. Then back here for a research break, I think."

"Looking up more cute small towns to film?"

"Yep. The hospitality angle has been the most popular with our test viewers so far, so the network wants to hunt down some more bed and breakfast renovations to feature."

"Sounds fun." Hopefully she sounded convincing. Nothing about Angelica's job actually seemed fun. Naomi had gotten her fill of constant travel years before.

Angelica laughed. "Nice try."

Naomi grinned at her friend. "I have no idea what you like so much about being on camera."

Angelica shrugged. "I'm good at it, and these days, I get to do it by being myself and talking about something I love instead of having to be some other actress's fake best friend or the girl who dies in the first ten minutes of a movie."

"I liked that one," Noah observed. "You're a good die-er."

"Gee, thanks." Angelica rolled her eyes. "It took ages to get the fake blood out of my hair. I thought I was going to have to chop it all off." She tossed her head, golden waves bouncing gently off her shoulders.

Noah reached out and tugged a strand of hair. "It would have grown back."

"Not in time for 'Clueless.'" Angelica's biggest role had been in a remake of the teen classic. She'd played the awkward friend, Tai. Naomi had seen the movie well before she met Angelica, and she still marveled that the curvy, vibrant woman sitting across from her could ever have been that person on screen.

"Speaking of time…" It was her job to keep this conversation on track. "Think you'll have time during your research breaks for my buddy, here?" She waved vaguely in Noah's direction.

He rolled his eyes. "Smooth, Nay."

She shrugged helplessly. "I do what I can."

Angelica narrowed her eyes at both of them. "Is this a marry-me-Angelica intervention?"

Noah had the grace to look guilty. "Maybe."

"I can't believe you agreed to this, Naomi."

"He caught me at a weak moment!" she protested. "It's not my fault!"

"What kind of weak moment?" Angelica's gaze sharpened. "Maybe one having to do with Iain Brennan?"

Noah's head snapped around so fast Naomi thought his neck might break. Now she was the focus of *both* of their attention. She'd forgotten that couples in love sometimes turned into bizarre and frightening two-headed Cerberuses of judgement.

"What are you talking about?" Innocence was her best defense, but it wasn't really her strong suit.

"We all know you're sleeping with him, Nay." Noah raised his eyebrows at her. "Even if it wasn't obvious, Angelica took him *shopping.* You know what happens at Target doesn't stay at Target."

She raised her hands to ward off their stares. "So? I'm not allowed to have sex all of a sudden?"

Angelica snorted. "You can have all the sex you want, now that you're not having it with Noah." She stuck her tongue out, and the twinkle in her eye let Naomi know her friend was teasing. Mostly, anyway. There'd been a few awkward moments early in their friendship, but everything was on an even keel these days.

"I thought we were having an intervention here." Naomi pointed at Angelica and assumed an imperious expression. "You there. Get married. Et cetera."

"Nice try, Queen of the Commitment-Phobes. Let's talk about the fact that you're *still* sleeping with that Irishman." Angelica raised one perfectly shaped eyebrow.

"What are you implying?"

"That you're daaaaaaating him." Noah's singsong accusation made Naomi grit her teeth.

"We're not dating. We have an arrangement."

"Max says he barely even comes to the garage apartment."

"Not true. He's there right now, as far as I know." Naomi stuck her nose in the air, adopting her mother's no-more-talking face. "There you are. End of story."

Angelica snorted. "Hardly."

Naomi blew out a frustrated breath. "I definitely RSVP'd to the wrong intervention," she muttered.

"Come on, Naomi. We're your friends, and we all have eyes and at least a vague grasp of calendars. You never stay with the same guy this long." Noah narrowed his eyes at her. "You don't do relationships. You barely stick around to learn people's last names."

"So?" She didn't need to justify anything about her life to a man who owned as many flannel shirts as Noah did. He clearly wasn't all there.

"Nobody's judging you," Angelica said. "Frankly, I'm sometimes a little jealous of the action you get."

"Hey!" Noah protested.

"Hush." Angelica grinned. "She's been living her best life."

"True that." Noah shrugged. "But the thing is, Naomi, this seems different."

Angelica nodded. "I haven't known you that long, but even I can tell something is different." She glanced at her boyfriend. "Even Noah here has barely spent much time in your house, but Iain's there all the time these days."

"Please tell me you're not spying on me." Naomi

scowled at them. "You both have much better things to do than sit outside my house watching to see who goes in and out."

"Your neighbor is on the library board with Sean's mother. And Mrs. Amory likes me," Angelica said smugly.

"Mostly because you order so many breakfast pastries from their bakery." Noah's tone was dry.

"Well, that, and also I'm delightful."

Naomi put her hand to her forehead. "Sometimes I forget how small River Hill is."

"There are pros and cons," Angelica said sympathetically. "Everyone knows you, but everyone *knows* you, too."

Naomi nodded.

"Still glad you live here?" Noah asked.

She made a face. "Most of the time. At least my parents aren't here."

Noah and Angelica both laughed. Noah had known Naomi's parents all his life, and Angelica had met them recently at an event she'd hosted on behalf of the network that aired her show. Noah had made a point of introducing her to Naomi's mother, which had in turn made Naomi's phone nearly explode with text messages and voicemails alternately insinuating that she ought to steal him away and suggesting that she "get over him" by going out with one of the sons of her mother's society friends. There was a list. Her mother had emailed it to her. Twice.

"So, is Iain moving in with you, or what?" Noah reached across Angelica for the basket of pastries Naomi had brought as her contribution to dinner.

"No!" Naomi exclaimed. "God, Noah, we're just sleeping together, and we hang out sometimes. Get over it."

Noah leaned forward, concern knitting his eyebrows together. "He's got a hard stop on being around, you know. Back to Ireland in less than six weeks. Plane tickets in hand. This is the closest I've seen you come to being in an actual relationship since you were twenty, Nay. I just don't want to see you getting hurt."

"We don't want either of you to get hurt," Angelica said. "Iain's a nice guy."

"I'm aware of that. And I know you both mean well, but the implication that I'm going to wither up and die when he goes home is fairly insulting." Naomi kept her tone as even as she could manage. "I'm an adult. So is Iain. Not that it's any of your business, but I'm sure you'll be relieved to know that we did in fact talk it over and agree to hang out together until he leaves. It's already dealt with."

Noah and Angelica exchanged glances, communicating silently in some sort of couple telepathy. Naomi resisted the urge to roll her eyes.

"So you're not going to start doodling your name and his all over your notebook?" Noah stuffed another half a pastry into his mouth as he spoke, and the last few words came spraying out with an extra helping of crumbs.

"Could you be more disgusting? No." Naomi looked at the table. "I was going to volunteer to help clean up, to thank Angelica for cooking, but if you're going to say-and-spray, you just signed yourself up."

Angelica chuckled. "That seems fair." She looked back

at Naomi, a thoughtful frown crossing her face. "Can I ask you a rude question?"

Naomi threw up her hands and leaned back in her chair. "Why stop now? Go for it."

"What are your future plans?" Angelica clasped her hands on the table in front of her as Noah gathered the empty plates and carried them to the sink.

Something about the other woman's posture niggled at Naomi's brain, but she couldn't quite put her finger on it. Not while warning bells were sounding in her head. Anytime someone asked what she had planned for the future, the discussion inevitably turned to what a disappointment she was or how she wasn't living up to her God-given potential. Her potential being, of course, to become a doting wife and mother.

"What do you mean?" she asked, even though she wasn't sure she wanted to know.

"I mean personally."

Naomi felt her eyebrows rising. "Wow. Have you been talking to my mother?"

Angelica pursed her lips. "I'm just curious. I was talking to Iain about the same thing the other day."

Naomi felt her stomach drop. Here came the words. Iain wanted a dozen babies and a perfect wife who would drive them around to all their baseball practices and piano lessons. No, he was moving back to Ireland. Rugby practice? Harp? No wonder he had freaked out about the condom.

"I don't want kids," she said quickly. *Best to get it over with.*

A familiar silence descended on the room. It was the

awkward quiet of people whose worldview included the ever-present assumption of future children when confronted with somebody who didn't fit in. She recognized it, because she'd caused it often enough.

"At all?" Angelica finally asked.

"At all." Naomi kept her tone firm. Years of having this conversation made it a lot easier. And at least Angelica and Noah would listen to her, and maybe even believe her, unlike her family. "I'm not interested. I like being an aunt, but I have never once wanted kids of my own. Frankly, I'm getting really excited to turn thirty-five in a couple of years. My sister-in-law says that's when the doctors think your ovaries dry up, and people stop bothering you about it." Angelica and Noah exchanged glances again, but Naomi plowed on. "If Iain told you he wants kids, that's fine. Just another reason two months is plenty. Great sex, no strings." She smiled at them. "It's okay to be jealous."

Angelica giggled. "Only a little."

Noah bonked her on the head with the empty pastry basket on his last pass to clear the table. "You're not funny."

"I'm hilarious." Angelica beamed at him. "You love me."

"I do love you. Strings and all." He leaned in for a kiss, and Naomi took the opportunity to make her escape.

"Thanks for dinner," she said as she stood up. "You can practice your cooking on me anytime, Angelica."

"Be careful what you're asking for," Noah said.

"Hush, you." Angelica rose and walked Naomi to the door. "Thanks for coming." She gave Naomi a quick hug. "It's always good to see you." She let go and opened the door for Naomi to leave. "Maybe you can bring Iain next time."

"Maybe," Naomi said. "If he's still around."

It wasn't until she was driving away that she realized Angelica had completely avoided the marriage question by turning the 'intervention' right back around to Naomi and Iain. Maybe that little conversational gambit hadn't been quite so altruistic after all. She'd *known* something was off about the way Angelica had posed her question, but she'd been too preoccupied with smoothing down her own ruffled feathers to see clearly what she'd been trying to accomplish. Score one for Angelica.

"Clever woman," she murmured. And immediately began plotting revenge. She was definitely going to sign Angelica up for gift subscriptions to at least three bridal magazines the *second* she got home.

14

Coming up on the sign that heralded the exit toward River Hill, Iain let out a long, satisfied sigh. He'd been working non-stop for the past two weeks. Al those long hours on the road had finally begun to pay off.

For the past few days he'd seriously wondered if this whole scheme was mad. The contract tucked safely away in his briefcase proved otherwise. The order for five hundred bottles of Whitman's Revival for a new speakeasy-style restaurant in Oakland was an excellent start.

A start he felt like celebrating. And he knew exactly how he wanted to go about doing that.

Trudging up the side staircase that led to his tiny one-room apartment over Max's garage, Iain loosened his tie and yanked it off over his head as he walked through the door. He dropped his bag next to the rickety chair in the corner, kicked off his shoes, and made his way to the bathroom for a quick shower to wake him up as much as refresh his tired body.

Twenty minutes later, he stepped out of the shower to check his phone and saw the message he'd been waiting for. Gavin Crawley, a musician he knew from back home, had been touring the U.S., playing small, intimate venues. Tonight he had a gig in Santa Rosa. Iain didn't love the idea of more time in the car, but if he could convince Naomi to join him, the long drive would be worth it.

Things had been great between them lately. When they weren't working, they were either eating or fucking, and if it hadn't been for the stress of his job, he could truthfully say the past couple of weeks had been outstanding. There was something very freeing about being with a woman who had no expectations of forever.

And he knew Naomi felt the same. She'd said as much yesterday morning after waking him up with her lips wrapped around the head of his cock. When she finished getting him off, she'd chuckled and then whispered something about their non-relationship being "the best idea ever."

Iain was sure he'd look back on their time together with a mixture of lust and fondness. The only downside was he didn't know if he'd ever find someone else who would be able to get him going quite the way Naomi managed to.

But tonight, he wanted to get *her* going. He knew his whiskey was damn good, but the restaurateur had called out its branding as being an essential element of why he'd gone with Whitman's instead of a more well-known commodity.

The label Naomi had designed fit the aesthetic of the new restaurant perfectly, and because of how well it tied with the space's overall look, Whitman's would take pride of place in the circular bar area smack dab in the middle of the room. In fact, the chef was going to have his bartender create a whole series of signature cocktails featuring Whitman's. Iain knew he owed a large part of this deal to Naomi's ingenious work, and he wanted to thank her. Properly. He picked up his phone and opened the text messaging app.

Iain: Remember how you said we should order Chinese and stay in tonight?

He sat back against his headboard and waited for Naomi's response. He knew she'd been sculpting all day, and if his timing was correct, she should be wrapping up soon. The light in her studio was best in the morning; the shadows caused by the late afternoon sun filtering through the large oak tree outside her window could be problematic if she was working on some of the more intricate parts of one of her designs.

As predicted, her response wasn't too long coming. Three dancing dots appeared on his screen before they were replaced with her reply.

Naomi: I've been looking forward to dumplings all day.

He smiled fondly. She was an unapologetic hedonist—something he adored about her, since it matched his own voracious appetites so well.

Unfortunately for her though, Iain had something other than dumplings in mind. From any other man, at any other time, what he was about to propose would probably sound suspiciously like a date. Thankfully, they were well past all that nonsense.

Iain: How about the best tacos in Santa Rosa and a concert instead?

Naomi: Santa Rosa? If you want tacos, you should swing by Max's on your way over here, then I can still have my dumplings.

Okay, maybe the tacos shouldn't have been his opening gambit. All of his new friends were seriously obsessed with Max's carnitas, seemingly to the exclusion of all other attempts at the dish. Iain was pretty sure Noah was close to petitioning the city council to make them the official food of River Hill, and the rest of them weren't much better. On the plus side, she hadn't said no to the outing—just his choice of meal. He could still salvage the situation.

Iain: How about you order your beloved dumplings, and you can eat them in my car? I have a buddy playing a gig that I want to check out. Plus, I'm celebrating.

Naomi: You got a sale?!?

Iain: I did. That new place in Oakland I was telling you about the other day. They loved the label, so naturally, I wanted to include you in my celebrations. I couldn't have done it without your help.

Naomi: Well, why didn't you say so? I'd love to!

Iain: Pick you up in thirty?

Naomi: Better make it forty-five, if that's okay?

Her response was immediately followed by the second selfie she'd sent him that day—unlike the one she'd sent this morning, however, her glasses were long-gone, and her dark hair was covered in a fine dusting of clay powder. And his black button-down? He was pretty sure it belonged to Naomi now. No way was he ever going to be able to get those stains out. He waited for the annoyance to come, but it never did. *Interesting.* He'd once dated a girl who'd stolen one of his shirts much as Naomi had, and that stunt had signaled the end of their relationship. But seeing *this* woman clad in nothing but his shirt? He liked it.

Christ, she's sexy, Iain thought, his thumbs brushing over the virtual keyboard. "See you then," he typed, and then set his phone to the side to finish getting dressed.

Later, he wouldn't have been able to explain why he'd taken the time to remove the wrinkles from his clean shirt with the iron Angelica had made him pick up at Target. All Iain knew was that looking good for Naomi wasn't the chore it would have been with anyone else.

And he wasn't going to examine too closely why that was.

"Your friend is amazing." Naomi linked her arm through Iain's as they strolled toward his car at the far end of the lot. "Thank you for bringing me."

Traffic had been terrible getting down to Santa Rosa, and Iain had been worried they'd miss the start of Gavin's show, but seeing the relaxed smile on Naomi's face made their mad dash worth it. He would never admit it aloud, but he enjoyed being the one to make her light up like this. She frequently wore a cynical scowl instead of the smile that transformed her face; Iain knew it was generally due to something her mother had said about the choices Naomi made. It made him happy to know he could give her a few moments of respite from all her familial expectations.

That was yet another thing they had in common. Iain always felt guilty complaining to any of his friends back home, but he didn't worry about Naomi judging him. While their families were worlds apart—literally—she just *got it*. She understood how hard it was for Iain to live up to his father's expectations, and how frequently he was compared to his two older brothers. Probably because she was in the same situation.

Cathal Brennan would like nothing more than for Iain to come home and settle down with a nice Irish girl who'd give them lots of grandbabies—exactly as his brothers had done. And Naomi's mother? Well, he'd overheard enough of Naomi's conversations with the woman to know she wanted her daughter to settle down with a successful Jewish doctor. Someone exactly like her brother. It was no wonder Iain and Naomi got along so well—they were practically the same person.

"You're welcome," he said, dropping a quick kiss on her lips before opening the passenger side door for her. When they were both settled in their seats, he pulled out of the lot and onto the freeway, back toward River Hill.

"Want the last dumpling?" she asked, tilting the box of cold Chinese food his way.

"No thanks. I know you want to finish them."

Naomi popped it into her mouth and smiled. When

she swallowed, she said, "You know me too well, Mr. Brennan."

Iain's chest pinched tightly, and he rubbed the ache away with the heel of his palm.

"You okay?"

He nodded and flicked his eyes her way. "Yeah, just a twinge. Probably your dumplings." He winked, but even as he said it, the words rang false in his mind. Iain had a stomach made of lead. You had to, when whiskey was your lifeblood. He could drink loads of the stuff and never suffer heartburn or acid reflux—an unfortunate side effect of whiskey for some. Maybe Mr. Chin's had used a new spice in their dumpling filling that he wasn't used to.

Whatever it was, he didn't like the feeling—at all. It was like someone had wrapped their fist around his heart and then squeezed with all their might.

Naomi rooted around in her purse. "I think I have an antacid in here somewhere. There!" She pulled out a silver foil-wrapped tube and passed it his way.

Iain plucked a tablet out of the wrapper and popped it in his mouth. *Eww, disgusting.* "Thanks," he said, swallowing down the chalky substance that coated the inside of his mouth like a grotesque mixture of sawdust and toothpaste.

"No problem. I'm not a huge heartburn girl, but if I'm feeling stressed about something, the acid in my stomach builds up, and it just fucking hurts." She laid her hand on his thigh and squeezed. "And I know you've been carrying the weight of the world on your shoulders lately."

"Yeah, that must be it," Iain answered idly, rubbing the spot above his left pectoral when it clenched again. Until this afternoon, he'd been worried he'd have to return to Dublin with his tail tucked firmly between his legs to a loud chorus of 'I told you so.' This whole thing—trying to launch an unknown brand, and in California of all places—had been *his* idea. He'd put his *and* Maeve's reputations on the line, and if things didn't work out, they'd never hear the end of it. Failure was *not* an option.

Naomi twisted in her seat to better face him as he guided his car down the freeway off-ramp toward her cottage at the edge of River Hill's town limits. "How long have you known Gavin?"

Iain was thankful for the change in topic. Thinking about what his father would say if his gamble didn't pay off made him moody, and he didn't want to brood. He wanted to enjoy the rest of the evening with the beautiful woman at his side. "We went to school together," he answered, a fond smile stretching his lips as he turned onto Naomi's street. "We were in a band together, if you can believe it."

"No way!" She bounced animatedly in her seat. "You've never mentioned you're a musician." Abruptly, the excitement dimmed from her eyes, and she looked out the window as he pulled into her driveway.

Briefly, Iain wondered if she'd come to the same conclusion about that statement he had. He hadn't ever mentioned he could play the guitar because that wasn't what their relationship was about. They only talked about the present—he told her about his difficulties making a sale, and she explained how the sculpture she was currently working on was fighting her—but they never really got into their pasts. Or, for that matter, their futures. Almost as if they had an unspoken agreement not to bring up something that might make this ... something more.

Naomi pushed open the car door, and he came around the back of the vehicle to take her hand. Brushing aside their awkward moment, he lifted her knuckles to his mouth. "I can play guitar. Not as well as Gavin, but I can carry a tune."

They reached her door, and he dropped her hand. Setting the key in the lock, she twisted it, and the door snicked open. They stepped over the threshold and, as if moving by instinct, Iain moved behind her to help her with her coat. They did this so often now that it was almost second nature. And *that* was a thought that didn't need exploring.

"Can you sing, too?" she asked, dropping her keys in a bowl on a low, mission-style table and kicking off her heels. He shook his head in a negative as she headed toward the kitchen at the back of the house. "Oh, well. Drink?"

"Thanks," he mumbled, unwinding the scarf from around his neck and hanging it on the peg next to her jacket. He removed his coat and hung it up as well, pausing a beat to stare at their clothing hanging side by side, the pain in his chest making itself known again.

He shook his head to try and banish the strange thoughts that were buzzing around in his head like a swarm of angry bees. He liked Naomi; they got along really well. And hell, he loved fucking her, that went without saying.

That's all this is, he told himself. And he really wanted

to believe that, but he couldn't help but wonder if maybe he wasn't developing … *feelings* for her. Unwanted, inconvenient feelings.

They'd made a deal, damn it, and he had every intention of upholding their bargain. Brennan men always kept their word, and he'd promised Naomi this wouldn't happen. He needed to shut this down, and fast.

Iain stared at his reflection in the mirror hanging next to the door. "Get yourself together, man," he scolded his scowling expression. He took a deep breath and squared his shoulders. Running a hand over his artfully-mussed hair, he caught his eyes one last time before turning away. From all outward appearances, he was still the same guy he'd been earlier that day. He could go on pretending that nothing had changed, that something about the seemingly simple domestic routine of returning to Naomi's home together like they'd done it a million times before hadn't thrown him for a loop.

It was probably just Gavin's music getting to him. His friend had unveiled a new song tonight about falling in love with someone you'd only ever considered a friend. It was about a girl back home they'd both known since they were teenagers; Iain still couldn't believe the two had hooked up, much less fallen in love. The world truly worked in mysterious ways.

He stepped into the kitchen to find Naomi at the counter muddling a sugar cube with bitters for an old fashioned. Dropping a twist of orange peel on top, she passed the glass to him. "Cheers on your sale."

They clinked glasses, and he took a sip. "Mmm, that's good."

She smirked. "You're just saying that because I used your family's whiskey."

Iain winked. "I know you did."

She tilted her head to the side and stared at him with a look of intense concentration. "*How* did you know? I put it in a decanter so you wouldn't."

He glanced at the decanter in question, and realization dawned. Naomi didn't drink whiskey, but he'd gotten her to try it by mixing up one of his favorite cocktails. He'd never noticed *this* decanter before now, though. And the bottle of whiskey he'd brought over last week wasn't one of his family's—it was a lighter blend from a distiller about an hour south of River Hill that was good for beginners. At some point, Naomi had gone shopping *specifically* for Brennan's whiskey. He didn't know what that meant, but it did … things to him.

Gave him feelings he didn't want to have. Made him have thoughts he shouldn't be having.

Iain set the glass on the counter and stepped toward her. Placing his hand to Naomi's waist, he pulled her closer until their thighs touched. She looked up at him and licked her lips. Lips he wanted to kiss. Lips he wanted to get lost in. "I have a very refined palate, Miss Klein. Allow me to demonstrate."

His lowered his head and captured her mouth in a long, slow, drugging kiss. One, Iain hoped, would drown out the angry buzzing that was back in his head.

15

___

Brrrrt. Brrrrt. Naomi opened one eye and peered at her phone, vibrating anxiously on the nightstand.

"Are you going to get that?" Iain mumbled from her other side.

"No. It's just my mother. Probably wants to give me the schedule of events I'm supposed to attend for the next two weeks." She rolled over and threw her arm over Iain's chest, snuggling in to him. "Not urgent in the least."

"Mmm. I can think of something urgent."

She let her arm drift downward. "Oh, my, this *is* an emergency."

He pinned her hand against him, and then used it to stroke himself. "You know it."

She giggled and tugged her fingers free of his hold, then pulled him toward her, using the momentum of his roll to bring him on top of her. "Let's see what we can do about that." Her last word came out on a gasp of pleasure as he tested her readiness with one of his long fingers, and then entered her in a slow thrust.

After that, they didn't talk about anything for a long while.

***

Over the next few days, they fell into an easy routine. Sex (so much sex), working, and the occasional outing in River Hill, to dinner at Frankie's or coffee at the Hollow Bean. On the days when Iain was on the road, driving up and down the coast securing contracts for Whitman's, Naomi worked furiously on the sculpture in her studio, carving the tiniest details into the growing form on her bench. It was nearly done.

So was their time together—something she was trying not to think about. It felt too good having him here, and spending time together in all her usual haunts. She couldn't let the swiftly approaching deadline of his departure make her sad; if she did that, she'd have to acknowledge how happy she was to be with him. And they'd agreed that this wasn't a relationship. If they weren't dating, she couldn't be heartbroken when he left. Simple.

On the days when Iain didn't need to meet in person with restaurant and bar owners, he set up shop in her home office. She cleared off one side of the long desk for him without being asked, shrugging when he raised an eyebrow in silent question.

"It's mostly old design projects. I've been meaning to file them anyway." She pointed to the nearly-empty bookshelf on the opposite wall. "They're supposed to be in binders over there, not spread out everywhere."

"You've made a lot of progress on that," he teased. There was exactly one binder on the shelf.

"For that, you can help me sort." She handed him a stack of glossy prints, and they settled down together on the floor to sort the papers by project.

"Thanks for doing this," he said. "Max's garage apartment is awesome, and the price is right, but it doesn't really have a lot of space for doing business."

She laughed. "I've been there once or twice. You could balance a fax machine on top of the bike trainer, maybe."

He chuckled. "He was gracious enough to let me move the exercise equipment, but I'm sure he's looking forward to having it back soon."

They both sobered at the reminder of their limited time, and Naomi gathered up the remaining papers awkwardly. "Well. Thanks. I needed to get this done."

He passed her his sorted stacks wordlessly, and she piled them onto the bookshelf to wait for their binders before fleeing back upstairs to the studio.

---

*T*wo days later, he came bursting in the front door as she sat frowning at her computer, putting the final touches on Max's menu design.

"I did it!" He tossed his briefcase onto the table in the hall and loped into the office, spinning her around in her desk chair to soundly kiss her.

Her arms twined around his neck and she lost herself

in his lips for a few minutes before she remembered what he'd said. "Did what?" she asked, rolling away.

"Met my sales goal," he said. "Come back. Don't stop." He tugged her back towards him, but she resisted.

"Iain! That's incredible!" She beamed at him. "I knew you would."

He blew out a breath that sounded like half of a laugh. "I'm glad one of us did. I was getting worried. There's not much time left on my father's deadline."

"Tell me everything," she ordered as she stood up. "Are you hungry?"

"Mm. I can't decide what I want first. Tacos, or you." His eyes roamed over her, and she felt her body warm quickly under his gaze.

"Well, unless you plan on wrapping me in a tortilla—" she held up a finger as he opened his mouth. "No!" She laughed. "That's not a thing. I vote tacos first, then some naked celebrating."

"Your motion carries," he said. "Get your jacket."

Over dinner, he told her about his day, barely able to restrain his jubilation. "You were right about the branding," he said. "One hundred percent. Thank you for putting it together. It keeps sealing these deals. Having the full package makes Whitman's seem like its own thing, not just some weird experiment from the Brennans."

"All three restaurants are placing orders?" She started on her second taco. "That's so awesome."

He nodded. "They all signed on, and it took me over the edge. Just in time."

"So now what?"

He leaned back in his seat, laying a hand across his

belly as he used the other to push his empty plate toward the center of the table. "Some of it depends on what my family says when I talk to them tomorrow, but I'm hoping the next step is expansion. Whitman's is a solid brand, and we're well on the way to having a real foothold here, so we could keep going."

Naomi set her taco down and eyed him. "What does keep going mean?" She wasn't entirely sure what the flutters in her stomach meant, but she probably shouldn't keep eating.

He looked thoughtful. "Well, presumably more sales trips now and again at the very least. A permanent directorship for yours truly." He rubbed his hands together. "I'm not talking fame, fortune, and glory, but at least I wouldn't be reporting directly to my older brother anymore. I could keep building this brand up, make it into something really well-known, you know?"

She nodded. His pride in himself and Whitman's Revival was evident in everything about him—his voice, his posture, his smile. "Do you think, um, you would be coming back here?" She couldn't believe she was asking. Their time together was nearly over, and here she was begging for more? But somehow, she found herself waiting breathlessly for his answer ... like it was going to change her life.

He leaned back in, his gaze suddenly intense. "Maybe. Would you want me to?"

"I mean ... if your job brought you here ... I wouldn't object to ..." she trailed off, unsure of what to say.

"A booty call?" He raised an eyebrow playfully.

She felt herself relax. "Yep. That. Definitely that. Your

booty. My booty. Together. Doing stuff." She made a circle with her thumb and forefinger and poked her opposite forefinger through it a few times for visual emphasis.

He laughed. "You're a true romantic, Miss Klein."

"I know," she deadpanned. "It's all those romance novels Angelica makes me read."

Angelica had developed a taste for historical romance novels during her Hollywood years. Naomi still wasn't sure how her friend had gotten hooked, although she'd once muttered something about Gwyneth Paltrow while Naomi was browsing the Oakwell Inn's well-stocked bookshelves.

Personally, she hadn't enjoyed the historical romances Angelica had foisted on her—it was a little difficult to read about a time when your ancestors weren't treated particularly well, while more dukes and duchesses than could possibly have ever existed trotted about never getting syphilis no matter how much 'rake reforming' they did.

But she'd found a few modern romance authors who were tackling more realistic pictures of historical life, and then she'd discovered contemporary romance, which had led to a month of solid reading. Now, Angelica was considering forming a River Hill book club, and she'd been badgering Naomi to join.

"You'll have to recommend one to me."

She raised her eyebrows at him, then lowered them and narrowed her eyes. "Challenge accepted." She leveled a finger at him. "Get ready to have your mind blown."

"I'm so ready. I mean, my mind, of course, and at least one other part of my body, right?"

She let her head fall back as she laughed. She really enjoyed being with Iain, more than she'd ever expected to. None of the other men she'd spent time with had ever been as good at dirty banter as he was, and none of them had ever enjoyed it very much when she'd made saucy comments. Iain not only liked it, but he was happy to engage her competitive side in a game of one-upmanship. Her conversations were going to be so much more boring once he left.

"Listen …" She didn't know what impulse made her open her mouth, but she found herself plunging on. "If you do come back here, for work, you could, um, stay at my place if you want." He was silent, and she realized she was actually blushing as she raised her eyes to meet his gaze. "Not that you have to. I just—"

"I would love to." He reached across the table and took her hand. "Are you sure? I just didn't expect you to say something like that, since … you know."

"Neither did I," she confessed. "It just popped out."

"That's what she said," he muttered under his breath.

She snorted. "I'm just saying, if it would be easier for you, I wouldn't mind." She paused. "We've been sharing the space pretty successfully, right? If you came to town for a few days here and there I think I could handle it."

"Good lord, I hope you'll do more than handle it," he said, waggling his eyebrows suggestively.

"You know I will," she laughed. "Any appendage you can think of."

"Thanks, Naomi." He squeezed her fingers, then turned her hand over to trace the lines of her palm with his own finger. "It means a lot. I know space is important to you."

"Don't get me wrong, you're still not allowed in the studio," she teased.

"I would never expect studio privileges. I'm not some kind of monster."

She laughed. "What do you think your family will say when you tell them you've met the quota?"

He let go of her hand and slid his palm back along the tabletop. "Really, you're going to bring my family into this lovely moment?"

"It's either that or we fuck right here on the table, and I think Max would get mad," she whispered conspiratorially.

"Fair enough. If you're going to kill my boner for Max's sake, I'll answer the question." He grinned at her. "Crisis averted. I don't know what they'll say for sure, but I'm hopeful they'll agree to my expansion ideas. At the very least, I expect they'll be pleased to see the business growth."

She narrowed her eyes. "Think your dad will be proud of you?"

He blew out a sigh. "Wishful thinking, but I hope so."

She grimaced. "I know the feeling."

"I know you do."

Right on cue, her phone buzzed against the hard surface of the table. Iain glanced down as the screen lit up and saw the long string of unopened text message windows. He raised his eyebrows. "That's a lot of texts."

"All from my mother."

He leaned over, reading a few of them upside down. "Are you going to answer her?"

She shrugged. "Definitely not right now. Maybe later. I don't know."

He reached over to steal her last taco. "Nothing urgent?"

"She wants me to come to more events this week, to help my dad secure the Chief of Medicine position he's gunning for. They think a united family front makes him look good, but they don't seem to care that I might have other stuff going on." She only had a little more than a week left with Iain; her family was going to be around for the rest of her life. She deserved a break. "My dad's a really good doctor, and he's well-liked in the hospital and in the community. If he can't get the damn job himself, maybe he isn't ready for it." Saying the words out loud felt disloyal, and she winced.

"Harsh truths," Iain observed around a mouthful of pork.

She sighed. "I told my mom about the Z Gallery deal and she didn't even register it. I could have told her about my deadline, and the fact that I legitimately have to work, but she wouldn't have believed me. It's easier this way."

Her phone buzzed again, this time with a new email and a voicemail notification. She hit the power button on the side to make it go dark again. She deserved some freedom, a little more time with Iain and her work. Which meant a few more days of ignoring her family. What was the worst that could happen?

*I*ain opened up his laptop and set it on the tiny coffee table in front of him. Launching his video chat app, he waited for the call to connect. He shouldn't be nervous—not with the great news he had to share—but he'd woken up this morning with a pile of lead resting heavy in his belly, and he hadn't been able to shake it.

Finally, his father's face appeared on the screen. When his oldest brother Braden's face moved into the frame next to their father's, Iain stifled a groan. *This can't be good.* He hoped his skepticism wasn't immediately evident to both men. If they sensed any weakness, they'd pounce. They weren't bad people; that was just the way it was between the men in his immediate family. Sometimes they reminded him of the pack of wolves he'd once watched a documentary about.

"Hey, man," his brother said, turning this way and that to admire his reflection in the camera feed, and the newly-grown beard that lined his jaw. One would think

Braden was the first man in the family to have gone this route. Iain had been sporting a beard for years, and all he'd ever gotten for it were un-funny hipster jokes.

"Hey, Dad. Hi, Braden."

"Thanks for getting up so early to do this call," his dad launched in. "I know the time zone differentials can be tricky."

"No worries. I've actually been up for hours." What Iain didn't say was that he'd rolled out of Naomi's bed at six o'clock this morning so that he could get back to his place, shower, and prep for this meeting. He'd had all his ducks in a row for a few days now—facts and figures at the ready—but he'd still wanted to make sure everything was airtight. This call could set the course of his life for the next several years. He needed to be at his best.

His dad nodded. "That's good. Used to be getting you up before half-ten was an exercise in futility."

"Used to be my job meant I was at the pub until they closed," Iain reminded him. Before he'd taken on the task of setting up the distillery's visitor center in Dublin, Iain had been responsible for the company's community outreach program. It basically meant he'd traveled around Ireland making sure Brennan's held pride of place in all the best bars, restaurants, and dance clubs. That meant late nights, and oftentimes, killer hangovers. Cozying up to the barbacks and pub owners had literally been in his job description, and still, he'd somehow caught flack for it.

But the past wasn't what this conversation was about, even if his father felt the need to take every opportunity to bring it up. It was time to look to the future, and how

Whitman's could play a significant role in the expansion of the Brennan stable of whiskey offerings abroad.

Eschewing further small talk, Iain launched right into the results of the last few months spent on the west coast. "I've got great news for you," he said, swiping his sweaty palms up and down his jean-clad thighs. "Not only have I hit my quota; I've surpassed it. All with two weeks left on the clock." He smiled and waited for the praise to come.

When instead his dad and his brother glanced meaningfully between themselves, he felt his smile dimming. He knew that look. He'd been on the other end of it for practically his whole life.

"What?" he asked, trying to keep his tone from turning belligerent.

"Son," his dad began, letting out a long, protracted sigh. A sigh that sounded an awful lot like the ones Iain had frequently heard as a kid.

But dammit, he wasn't a kid anymore, and this was his livelihood. "Don't 'son' me," he said, clenching his hands into fists at his side. "I'm not a child. I'm one of your employees, and a damn good one at that." He cast a pointed glare at his brother.

No one in the family liked to mention it aloud, but sales of Brennan's had been flat since Braden took over as CEO. Iain strongly believed it was because his brother lacked the vision needed to take the company where it should be.

It was an excellent time to be in the distilling business: sales of Irish whiskey were booming in the U.S., based largely on high-end premium offerings. Unfortunately, under Braden's leadership, Brennan's had been the last of the Irish distillers to offer a premium bottling, and their earnings reflected it. They were one of the oldest family-owned distilleries in Ireland. They ought to be at the top of every list, not scrambling to keep up.

Braden rolled his eyes and glanced away, muttering something about his youngest brother flying off the handle. Iain took a deep breath to calm his pulsing frustration. At the end of the day, as President of the company—and the person with the largest share of voting rights—only his father's opinion really counted. His oldest brother might like to *think* he was in charge, but Iain owned exactly as much Brennan stock as Braden and Fionn did, and in terms of voting rights, the two had no more say than Iain did.

His father blew out a breath. "No, you're not a child any longer, but your behavior these past few years *has* been childish. This is a family business, and you seem to keep forgetting that. This isn't the Iain show, where you get to prove what a maverick you are by striking out on your own. There's a way we do things here—a way we've always done things—and if you want to continue to be part of that, you need to learn to toe the party line. It's what's best for the brand, and what's best for the family."

A sickening feeling of dread settled low in Iain's gut. He had a sneaking suspicion he knew what the next words out of his father's mouth were going to be, but he asked for clarification all the same. "What are you saying?"

"I'm saying that this little experiment is over. You need to come home."

Home.

To a place where he would always play third fiddle;

where he was the punchline to a family joke; where a grown man was spoken to like a recalcitrant child. Nothing about that sounded appealing.

"And if I don't?" he pressed, holding his breath. Never, in the history of ever, had Iain ignored a direct edict from the Brennan family patriarch. He might have bristled over the years at the heavy-handed way his father dictated to him, but until now, he'd never felt the need to push back —too hard.

His brother's eyes flashed with surprise, and he cast a quick glance toward their father. Cathal Brennan, however, never flinched.

"If you don't, I'll be forced to fire you. I've let you have your fun with a paid sabbatical, but all that ends with a single word from you."

"This hasn't been a sabbatical!" Iain responded hotly. "I've been working my goddamn ass off out here, turning up business for the company. How can you not see that?"

His father's jaw ticked. "A handful of restaurants mixing up cocktails with our whiskey doesn't constitute significant business, and you know that as well as anyone."

"Did you even look at the information I sent over?" Iain breathed through his anger. *A handful of restaurants,* his ass.

With the purchase orders he'd procured for Whitman's, Maeve's whiskey would add another million dollars of profit to their bottom line this year alone. A million fucking dollars. And *he'd* done that. So what if most of those orders would find his sister's whiskey going into signature cocktails of some sort? It was a start on the path to success. And a fucking good one, at that.

Sure, they could have launched in Ireland, but the market was already saturated. In America, they were unknown, but they had history on their side. They were a novelty that people would want. When the time came for Whitman's Revival to stand on its own, Iain knew it would.

"Why are you fighting this?" Braden's tone was the same as it always was. Faintly exasperated, and deeply patronizing.

Iain flicked his gaze from his father to his brother. "Why am I fighting this? I'm fighting it because we're lagging behind our competitors, and no one is willing to acknowledge that. Everyone but us has introduced an offshoot to market recently, to both critical and financial acclaim. Has no one in the marketing department shown you the figures for Roe and Co or Method and Madness? Oh wait, they have. Multiple times." He knew this, of course, because he was the head of marketing.

"That's an entirely different strategy," his father said, bringing Iain's gaze back to him.

"I know that," he answered. "I'm not an idiot—even though you seem to think I am."

His dad ran a hand through his hair, a sure sign of his obvious frustration with his youngest son. "No one thinks you're an idiot. Impulsive, maybe, but not stupid."

"Then stop treating me like I am." He leaned forward so his face was nearer to the screen. He didn't know why he did it, except he had a feeling that if he was somehow closer to them, they might actually listen. "In case you've forgotten, my last impulsive idea was named Dublin's top tourist attraction last year."

"*That* was a good idea," his dad conceded, "but *this* one isn't. At least not in its current form. Come home, Iain, and we'll figure out how to launch your sister's whiskey the right way. The Brennan way. This was never going to be something real, son. We never intended to expand in the direction you want."

The words hit Iain like physical blows. *It was never going to be real. Come home.* He stared at his dad and brother for several long seconds, the ultimatum hanging heavy between them. There it was. They'd never intended to support him. Either Iain abandon his work here and return to Dublin, or he could forget about any help from his family. *Dammit.* He knew he was on to something here, but he didn't know how successful he could be without the financial backing of the Brennan coffers. Going it alone was a scary proposition. Not to mention the fact that he didn't know how his sister felt about this news.

"Have you discussed this with Maeve?"

His brother shook his head in the negative, while his dad said, "She's our next meeting. I wanted to speak with you first, since I know Whitman's was your idea. Your sister would never have done something like this one her own." He nodded firmly, his complacence folding around him like an invisible shroud.

Iain bit back a sarcastic laugh. That comment alone showed just how little their father actually knew his only daughter. The idea to launch Whitman's in America with a man-on-the-street guerilla-style marketing campaign had been all Iain's doing, but it had been Maeve who had approached him about spinning off from Brennan's in the first place. She was just as tired of the condescending treatment from their family as he was. In Iain's case, it was because he was the youngest son; hers, because she'd had the audacity to be born female, but still a brilliant distiller.

Iain rubbed the back of his neck, the stirrings of a plan forming at the back of his mind. "When do you need my decision on this?"

Frankly, he already knew what he'd decided, but he needed to talk to Maeve before he showed his hand. If he could just buy some time, he might be able to put together a new plan for Whitman's—one that would take both his family *and* the industry by storm.

There was also the not insignificant matter of leaving Naomi behind before he was ready to. They might have started out as casual, but these last few weeks had felt anything but. Neither one of them was willing to put a label on it, but he'd grown to care for her, and he knew she felt the same way about him. She'd even said he could stay at her house when he came back! That was *not* nothing, especially for Naomi. The scariest part was that when she'd extended the offer, he'd been ready to say a whole hell of a lot more than "yes" and "thank you." A part of him had been tempted to tell her just how much it meant to him.

He'd thought he had the next two weeks to show her instead.

His family was *not* going to steal that away from him. They might try to stifle his vision where the business was concerned, but there was no fucking way he was going to let them stifle a relationship with the first woman he'd ever cared to use that word with.

His father was frowning, but Iain plunged ahead. "Because if it's all the same to you, I'd like to take the rest of my allotted time out here. You probably wouldn't understand, but I've made important contacts here, and friendships I'm not going to just walk away from because daddy wants me back at home." He crossed his arms over his chest, daring either of them to challenge him.

His father visibly bristled at Iain's tone, and he opened his mouth to speak, but then closed it. Turning away, he said, "Two weeks, then" and stabbed his finger onto the key that would end their call.

17

"Slow down. What do you mean?" Naomi cradled the phone between her head and shoulder as she tilted her neck at an uncomfortable angle. Her fingers held a tiny chisel, dangling loosely over her sculpture. She tightened her grip on the tool as she frowned. Iain's call had come at an unexpected time. She was elbow deep in clay, nearing the final turn on her race to finish the piece. Hands covered in dust and grime, she'd managed to answer the phone with her nose and pick it up with her wrists to get it near her ear. It was a move she'd perfected ages ago.

"I mean it's over, Naomi. They never had any intention of producing this blend full-time; just as a bit of a lark. My father says they were indulging me. He called what I've been doing out here a goddamn sabbatical."

"That's insane. You've been working your ass off." She scowled. Iain's father sounded like a dick.

"That's what I said. Not that they listened." His voice

was garbled by pure rage, a sensation she knew well when it came to dealing with family.

"What are you going to do?"

He sighed. "They gave me a choice. Either come home or get fired."

She felt her stomach drop, and barely rescued the chisel as it started to fall from her suddenly nerveless grasp. She placed the tool carefully on the workbench before she said anything. "Those seem like … tough options. I don't understand. I thought you'd met your quota."

"I did."

"But isn't that good? I saw some of those numbers. They were big orders."

"They were."

"I don't understand," she said again. Naomi knew she sounded less than eloquent, but this was the last bit of news she'd expected to receive, and it had her feeling a bit discombobulated—like she'd lived her whole life thinking the grass was green, only to suddenly learn it was actually orange. Her mind simply couldn't wrap itself around this new bit of information.

"It all boils down to the fact that they want all of the Brennans under the family thumb. Specifically, my father's thumb. My brothers have both bowed down, and I'm expected to do the same. So's Maeve."

"Wasn't this blend her production anyway?" They'd talked about it once, and his pride in his brilliant sister had shone through in every word he'd spoken. She thought it was sweet. Her brother had certainly never admired anything she'd done nearly so much. Jacob had grudgingly visited her a few times, only to make a few critical comments about her house. And he mostly ignored her art. Which was, for her family, basically great praise. The Kleins took 'if you don't have anything nice to say, don't say anything at all' as a challenge, not a guideline.

"Yes." There was a muffled noise on the other end of the line, as though he were rifling through a stack of papers. "I need … I need to talk to her."

"Have they spoken to her about this? From what you described of her, I can't believe she'd agree to this."

He grunted a negative. "Apparently, they wanted to break me down first. They think she'll be easier, and just knuckle under, I expect." He snorted.

"Do you have a plan?"

He was silent for a moment, and she pictured him running a frustrated hand through his hair. In her imagination, she reached out her own hand to smooth the tousled hair back down. "Not entirely. I need to talk to Maeve."

She swallowed. "Guess those work trip booty calls are off the table now, huh?"

He grunted. "Who knows? Maybe I'll be camped out on your doorstep sooner than you think."

Now *she* was the silent one, struggling for words. Was he going to quit his job? Their relationship—if that's what you could call it—was based entirely on the fact that they were two independent people with their own things going on. She had no intention of becoming a housewife, but she sure as hell didn't want a house husband, either. His family was forcing him to make an impossible choice, and whatever the two of them had going might not survive the fallout.

She didn't know what to say.

Apparently her silence dragged on too long, because his voice came back on the line, tentative and raw. "Naomi, I didn't mean—" He sighed, and to Naomi's ears it sounded sadly resigned. "I'm not going to show up at your door."

"I know," she said, then winced. "I mean, I don't know. You could."

"No, I couldn't. It's not like that between us."

He was right. It wasn't. She didn't want it to be, and neither did he. They had an agreement. So why did her chest ache so badly? "Okay. So, when do you leave?"

"I …" He paused. "I'm still on my schedule. Staying for the rest of my allotted time."

She felt her body thrum with anticipation, and maybe something else. "You're staying?"

"Through the last two weeks. I have some stuff to finish up. People to see."

Like her? God, she hoped so. The thought of him hopping on a plane back to Ireland tomorrow made her nauseated. They would still have their last few days together. After that … well. She shut down the thoughts she'd been letting creep through, little moments spent imagining them together later. Just as well. Getting attached was not part of the plan.

"Sounds good. I—" She was interrupted by the completely unexpected sound of her doorbell. "Iain! You're not here, are you?" She was halfway to the door, a delighted smile on her face when he answered.

"No. Why?"

Her smile died as she opened the door. "I, um, I'm going to have to call you back." Without another word, she hung up the phone and stared blankly at her visitor.

"Hello, darling," said her mother. "Aren't you going to invite me in? It's rude to leave your mother on the doorstep."

Naomi shoved her phone into her pocket, not sure which of the whirlwind of feelings blowing through her she should give in to. "Mom. Now isn't really a good time."

Judith Klein raised one elegant eyebrow and looked her daughter up and down. "Then why did you answer the door? You appear fully clothed, and it's the middle of the day, so I assume you're not up to anything inappropriate."

"Mother!"

"For heaven's sake, Naomi, you're in your thirties. If you haven't done anything inappropriate yet, you really should. Now let me in." Her mother stepped forward, and Naomi moved backwards without thinking.

"But—"

Her mother closed the door and held out her purse. "Where shall I put this? I assume you don't have a dedicated space in this … charming bungalow."

"There's a table right there." Naomi got the words out through gritted teeth. She knew exactly what her mother meant by 'charming. It was the real estate definition, and it wasn't flattering. She took the purse and resisted the urge to fling it roughly onto the table that rested against the stairs. Unfortunately, that would only break the bowl that sat there, a gorgeous piece she'd bought from a glass artist who lived down the road. Instead, she set the expensively logoed bag down gently and took a deep breath, letting it out slowly before she turned back to her mother.

"What brings you here?"

Her mother examined her surroundings. "Do you have a place to sit down?"

Naomi sighed. "Come on in. The living room is this way." The dining room had been converted to her office, but she'd furnished the cozy living room with a comfortable couch and a chair or two. She mostly used the space for watching ridiculous movies when she was feeling burnt out. Although she and Iain had done a few other things in there several days ago. Probably not something she should be thinking about as she watched her mother sit carefully down in the exact spot Iain had— never mind.

"So? You're sitting. In my house. Which you've never visited before, let alone showed up unannounced to. Why are you here, Mom?"

"Oh, it isn't just me, dear." Her mother smiled at her beatifically. "Your father's here, too. He's just taking a little nap. You know how travel tires him."

"You live less than two hours from here."

"Yes, of course. It was certainly a drive. There were many interesting fields and farms." Her mother's tone conveyed her opinion about such things, and it wasn't positive. "I left him at the cozy B&B we booked. So convenient that it had availability."

Oh, no. "You're staying? At a B&B?"

"Oh, yes. Even more charming than your little place here. I understand they've undergone some renovations recently."

"Mom, are you staying at the Oakwell Inn?"

"Well of course, darling."

"But that's Noah's—"

"Yes, I promised his mother a full report, of course." Her own mother sniffed. "Angelica is a charming girl, although she seems quite busy."

That explained why nobody had thought to warn Naomi about this ambush. Angelica was due to leave to film another segment of her popular show in a day or two. Possibly even tomorrow—Naomi wasn't sure of the exact schedule. But Noah and Angelica would have been far too busy cooing over each other to even register this particular emergency. They probably thought Naomi had invited her parents to come.

"Why are you and Dad here? You never leave the city."

"Darling, you didn't answer your phone. I assumed you were dead. We came to identify your body."

"You booked a B&B to identify my corpse?"

"Well, we certainly weren't going to stay at a Holiday Inn."

Naomi closed her eyes and sought patience. "You knew I wasn't dead. What's going on?"

Her mother leaned toward her. "It's an intervention, Naomi."

Naomi felt her jaw drop. "A *what*?"

"An intervention. Jacob and Tanya are on their way, too. We felt the whole family should be here."

Naomi's shoulders hunched involuntarily. This felt far

too much like *the talk* her family had given her during her sophomore year of high school, when she'd turned down a summer internship with a cousin's medical practice, electing instead to attend an art camp at Berkeley. She'd had a hard time standing up to them then. Only the promise that she'd apply to the universities of their choice the following year had smoothed it over. And her mandatory attendance at several hospital charity events, as if her parents needed to show the world that their daughter was still meek, proper, and obedient even if she did have a bohemian streak.

Was that what this was about? She straightened. "What kind of intervention, exactly? And for that matter, shouldn't you have waited for everyone else? Are you getting started early?"

"Well, I figured I'd get a jump start, since you and I are so close."

Naomi blinked. "Uh ..."

Her mother leaned back in her seat, then straightened with a twist of her lips. "Really, Naomi, you couldn't have gotten a firmer filling on these cushions?"

Naomi grinned. "I bought it second hand." She waited for the reaction. *In three, two, one ...*

Like clockwork, her mother practically leaped out of the chair. "Naomi Anne Klein! You let me sit on *used upholstery?*" She looked around wildly. "God knows what kind of vermin you let into your house! Have I taught you *nothing?* Oh, how are there no hard surfaces in here?" Her eyes searched the room frantically, and finding none, she folded her arms in front of her and visibly pretended that she wasn't itching all over. "I'll just stand."

"Worth it," Naomi whispered to herself, then raised her voice. "Relax, Mother, I bought it from a woman who never even used it. It sat in her living room covered in plastic until I took it off her hands. *And* I had it professionally sanitized." Her mother had, in fact, taught her that little tip. *Secondhand furniture is fine, but never upholstered.* She'd itched a little bit herself the first few times she'd sat on it, but after paying for it to be cleaned three more times, she'd finally felt comfortable with it in her house. She probably could have bought something brand new for the cost of all that cleaning but conquering her mother's voice in her head had been worth the price.

"Well, I'm not sitting on it." Her mother's chin firmed. "I'll just stand until your father gets here."

"I thought you said he was napping."

"Yes, Jacob and Tanya are picking him up when they arrive and coming straight here. We're all very worried about you."

"Worried? Why?"

"Naomi, you haven't answered your phone for weeks!"

"It's been, like, four days. Tops."

"I was sure I was going to read about your grisly murder in the newspaper."

"Ugh. First of all, who reads the newspaper? Do you at least have a digital subscription? Second of all, I'm *not dead*. I'm *busy*, Mom. There is a difference, you know."

Her mother sniffed. "Busy with what? What on earth could you possibly be doing out here in the country?"

Naomi threw up her hands. "Again! Two. Hours. Away. And I'm *working*, Mom! Remember? I have a successful art career?"

Her mother rolled her eyes. "I'm sure you do."

"Do you want to see the checks?" Naomi heard her own voice rising to a shriek. How did her mother always do this to her? "I have a *mortgage*!"

"Of course you do, dear. And a cell phone bill. Which I assume you pay with those checks. Which means that you could have answered your phone, but you didn't. Hence, why we're here." Her mother spread her hands, as if all had been resolved, then smiled patiently at Naomi. "I'm sure your father and brother will be here soon, and we can really get down to business."

Was it wrong to flee your own home? Naomi's phone buzzed in her pocket, one short vibration indicating a new text. She pulled it out and glanced at it.

Iain: Is everything okay? Do I need to come over there? What happened?

Her mother shifted slightly. "While we wait, I'm going to use your facilities." She glanced around. "Feel free to tidy up while I'm gone." She sashayed out of the room as if she owned the place, a signature Judith Klein move.

Naomi unlocked her phone and typed furiously.

Naomi: The reckoning has come. My mother is here. Save yourself. STAY AWAY.

18

Standing on the sidewalk outside the small regional airport in Santa Rosa, Iain's mouth split into a wide grin when his sister stepped out into the California sunshine. "I can't believe you came," he said, pulling Maeve into a hug.

"When my brother calls—the good one, mind—and says to get my arse to California, I'm there."

He rolled her carry-on luggage behind him as they made their way to his car. "You're here four nights, right?"

Angelica had offered up Iain's old room at the Oakwell Inn at a reduced rate. It was an added expenditure he hadn't anticipated—especially now that he was counting his pennies in anticipation of his family's censure—but the tiny space above Max's garage simply wasn't suitable for sibling slumber parties.

And there was no way Iain was going to ask Naomi to put his sister up, especially since everything between them felt a bit unsettled. Her statement about him not turning up on her doorstep had hurt more than he'd let on. Add to the fact that he hadn't heard from her in a couple of days, and he was left wondering where they stood. The last thing she'd said to him was to stay away, and he hadn't heard a peep since. He was trying not to worry.

"Three," Maeve clarified. "Mam thinks I'm at a hen do in Vegas."

"Smart."

"I needed to get away. Fionn's on one of his high horses, and Dad cornered me with the promise of my own project at Brennan's. Obviously, he hopes if he bribes me well enough, I'll get you to come over to the dark side."

Iain snorted and rolled his eyes as he pulled onto the freeway. It had only been forty-eight hours since his father had stabbed him in the back with the news that the family had no intention of producing Whitman's Revival no matter what he did. Since their call, Iain had received five different emails promising him all manner of promotions, hoping to get him to return to the family fold. He'd ignored them all.

What the old man hadn't counted on, of course, was that the two youngest Brennans were tired of being dictated to, and they'd swiftly hatched a plan to take control of their destinies. Or, at least, the beginnings of a plan. That's what had brought Maeve to California so quickly—to see if Iain's scheme had any merit.

"Do you want to go to Angelica's to take a nap, or head over to the distillery first?"

Maeve bounced in the seat. "The distillery!"

He should have known. Ever since he'd floated his new

idea past her, she hadn't been able to stop talking about it.

"I can't believe you found one that's for sale."

Neither could Iain. Truly, it had been a stroke of luck. A few tech bros had decided it would be cool to distill gin and vodka with their buddies. They'd invested in all the equipment but had quickly grown tired of the venture. Now they wanted out. Noah had found out about the fire sale through the grapevine—no pun intended—and had given Iain a call several days ago. Originally, he'd intended on proposing the facility to his family. Now, he wanted it to be his. His and Maeve's, rather. On paper, everything looked like it could work, but he needed his sister to inspect the stills before they'd know for sure.

Iain exited the highway and turned down a road leading into the small industrial part of town. It wasn't the prettiest section of River Hill, but they didn't need it to be. He wanted to make whiskey, not win beauty contests.

"I'm curious to see what you're going to think," Iain said, pulling into the driveway that led to a handful of warehouses. "I held off on checking it out in person until you could see it too."

"How come?" Maeve asked, hopping out of the car even before he'd put it in park.

Iain smiled fondly. After eighteen hours of travel, most people would be ready to drop, but not Maeve. She was like the Energizer Bunny when she was amped up on an idea. And this was a whopper of one. "You're the talent, remember?"

Iain entered the code into the security keypad and waited for the lock to disengage. When it did, he hefted the heavy steel door over his head with a grunt and stepped back to survey the space. The warehouse was over ten thousand square feet—well larger than what they'd need initially—but if things went well, they could grow into it.

"Well?" he asked.

Maeve turned to him, her jaw hanging open and excitement sparkling in her bright green eyes. "It's perfect, Iain. I couldn't have dreamed up a better distillery even if you'd asked me to."

"Are you sure? The stills are good?"

She nodded and lovingly ran a hand over the gleaming copper. "God bless tech bros who have more money than sense."

Iain laughed. "They claimed to have purchased 'only the best,' but you can never tell. How does some programmer know what type of still is best?"

"However they knew, they knew." She turned to face him but her hand continued to stroke the still's copper surface. "What's the next step?"

Iain blew out a breath. This was the part that made him nervous. He wasn't worried about himself so much. No matter what happened, he'd land on his feet. There were always jobs in tourism marketing to be had, but Maeve was another story. She hadn't gone to university, instead choosing to go to work directly in their family's distillery as soon as she was done with school. If their venture failed, what would happen to her?

As if sensing his unease, Maeve laid a hand on his arm. "Iain, stop worrying about me. I already told you, I'm in. You couldn't keep me away." She craned her head back to take in the long neck of the still. "I'm gonna need that big brain of yours to focus on how we're going to make it all work, not worrying about what happens to me if it doesn't. We can do this. We *will* do this."

Well, that settles that, Iain thought, wrapping his sister in another tight squeeze. Her faith in him never ceased to amaze him. She truly was the best damn person he knew, and if for no other reason than to make her a success, he vowed to do everything in his power to get their distillery up and running. "Now, sweet girl, I sell my shares in Brennans and we buy this place. I'll call the lawyers."

And then he'd wait.

Stay away. Iain stared at his phone. Naomi's directive had been clear, but that had been over seventy-two hours ago. Why the radio silence? Surely, her mom was gone by now.

Iain tried not to overreact, but truth be told, he was worried.

Iain: Everything good over there?

He waited for Naomi's reply to come, but when two more hours passed, he developed a bad feeling in the pit of his stomach. He and Naomi certainly didn't exist in each other's pockets, but they'd never gone this long without even a text exchanged between them, either.

His knee bounced up and down as he weighed his options. Sit here all night concocting scenarios in his head, or head on over to her place and risk interrupting something he shouldn't. Or worse.

What could be worse than not knowing? He cared

about Naomi, and if he was sticking around River Hill—
which it very much looked like he was now that he and
Maeve had put in an offer in to buy the distillery—he
needed to know where he stood with her.

Throwing his leather jacket on, Iain grabbed his keys
and bounded down the steps to his car. Ten minutes later,
he was parked at the curb in front of Naomi's house,
leaning to the side to inspect his surroundings through
the passenger-side window. Her car was in the driveway,
as were two others. None were marked "coroner," so he
supposed that was a good sign.

He drummed his fingers against the steering wheel. He
really didn't know what to do here. Naomi wasn't his
girlfriend. Hell, she'd explicitly told him to stay away. But
something about the situation didn't seem right, and if
something *was* actually wrong, he'd feel terrible for
having waited this long to check in on her. You didn't
leave people you cared about to fend for themselves when
they were in a bind.

Decision made, he made his way up her lavender-lined
walk. When he was about ten feet from her front door, he
heard voices. Loud voices. Iain paused, and then winced,
when he heard Naomi yelling something about Noah and
"his goddamned mommy issues."

He didn't know what *that* was about, but he *did* know
Naomi's parents had always assumed she and the grumpy
winemaker would end up together. He snorted. Clearly,
they didn't know their daughter—or Noah, for that
matter—if they thought those two were anything other
than a terrible idea. Naomi and Noah were more like a
bickering brother and sister than a couple, and sometimes

he wondered how they'd ever managed to get naked together. It made zero sense to him, but who was he to judge? Lord knew Iain had his own fair share of cringe-worthy partners in his past.

Stepping onto the first of three stairs that led up to her front door, Iain heard a male voice telling Naomi not to be so dramatic. *That is not going to go over well*, he thought with a smirk. In response, he heard Naomi telling the person to fuck off.

He paused, wondering if he should go any further. Clearly, she wasn't dead or in any sort of dire straits. At least physically. But if that was her family on the other side of her heavy wooden door, he knew she'd be livid. That was something they had in common. Three days spent with family who wanted you to be something you weren't was enough to drive anyone crazy. Now that he knew Naomi was still alive, he pulled out his phone to let her know she could escape to his place if she needed.

Iain: Hey, I'm outside. When I didn't hear from you, I got worried. Now that I can hear you're okay, I'll head out. Call me if you need to escape. I want to talk to you about something.

The something being his plans for sticking around River Hill. He'd planned to tell her about Maeve's visit and his idea, but then everything had gone sideways. As far as Naomi knew, he was only here for another week.

And she hasn't tried to contact you, a snarky voice inside his head chimed in. Not that he hadn't noticed. Her continued silence in spite of his looming departure date was probably the thing that bothered him most about all of this. Iain had thought that despite their promises not to get attached, they'd had something special building. Now, he couldn't help but wonder if it had all been one-sided. Regardless, he was sticking around, and she needed to know either way.

Iain turned to go when he heard the front door open behind him.

"Don't you dare leave me here to fend for myself," Naomi hissed as she galloped down the stairs to grab hold of his arm and spin him around. She planted a quick kiss on his lips, and then tugged him back up the stairs and through her front door to come face to face with the family he remembered meeting briefly nearly six months prior at the Founders' Ball.

"You all remember Iain?" she asked, shoving him forward and closing the door behind them.

Her mother tilted her head to the side to study him. "I don't believe so, no. How did you say you two know each other?"

"I didn't," Naomi said, crossing her arms over her chest and squaring off with her mom.

Iain hadn't remembered the two looking so much alike, but with twin expressions of annoyance on their faces, the resemblance was uncanny. Suddenly, he knew what Naomi would look like in thirty years—provided, of course, she visited the same plastic surgeon. Not that her mother's work was bad or anything, but no woman in her sixties looked like that naturally. At least not in his experience. His own mom looked fifteen years older than Naomi's.

"Wait, I remember you." Jacob Klein stepped forward. "You're the whiskey guy from the Founders' Ball."

"Iain Brennan. Guilty as charged." He grasped Naomi's brother's outstretched hand and shook it.

Stepping back, Jacob glanced back and forth between his sister and Iain, a slight smile tugging at his lips. "I didn't realize you two knew each other."

"We didn't; not at the time," Iain answered, unaware he'd said something he shouldn't have until Naomi elbowed him in the side and cursed his big mouth under her breath.

"Noah gave him my name when he needed someone to design a logo for his sister's whiskey," she rushed to add. No mention of the fact that they'd been seeing one another, or whatever it was they were doing, ever since.

Iain didn't know why, but that hurt. He was good enough to drag inside to interrupt what had clearly been a fraught family meeting, but he wasn't good enough to introduce as her friend. To acknowledge that he might even be something more? Her silence these past three days began to make more sense.

"Is that the one we tasted at the ball?" A man Iain recognized as Naomi's father stepped forward.

"Yeah. A friend of a friend hooked me up. He thought it might uncover some potential customers, but no luck." He shrugged. Iain had hoped the opportunity might lead to some big orders, but all that had resulted was in a dip in his inventory.

Judith Klein *tsked* at her daughter. "You didn't introduce him to Luis?

"Luis?" he asked, turning to face Naomi.

Before she could answer, Mrs. Klein stepped forward and led Iain to the sofa on the other side of the room. He paused briefly when she sat in the spot where he'd slowly and leisurely fucked her daughter the week before. Expecting to find a smirk on Naomi's face, he was shocked instead to see her lips flattened into a grimace and her cheeks scarlet with what looked like indignation.

Which, frankly, he didn't understand. His presence there was her doing. Sure, he'd come over uninvited even though she'd told him to stay away, but *she'd* invited him inside. Without looking at him, Naomi dropped into a chair in the corner, and went back to sulking.

Judith patted the cushion next to her, and Iain obediently sat down. "Luis Montero is the most prolific restaurateur in the Bay Area. He has ten restaurants right now, and is opening several more, all very nice. You may have seen him on the Food Network. He's been on some of their competition shows as a judge. Quite famous." She waved a hand airily. "He's a dear friend of the family. Naomi's known him her entire life." She turned to Naomi. "I'm sure he would have loved Iain's whiskey. Your brother and father did. Why didn't you make the introduction?"

Naomi lifted her chin in defiance. "You know how I feel about abusing personal connections for profit."

Judith rolled her eyes. "And you know that's just being naive. That's how business is done."

"Maybe in *your* world, but not in mine. In my world, I let the product speak for itself."

Judith set her hand to Iain's knee, a strange, proprietary gesture. Then again, she'd had to sign off on him peddling his wares at the Founders' Ball, so maybe she somehow felt responsible for his success—or lack thereof. "And Iain's whiskey speaks for itself. All you had to do was ask Luis to taste it, and he would have asked you to set up a meeting the very next day. You know he loves to have all the best stuff first. Honestly, Naomi. You'd better hope he doesn't find out you've been keeping this nice man a secret. He'll be very cross with you."

"I was not *keeping* a *man* a *secret*," Naomi hissed through gritted teeth. Even though as far as Iain could tell, that was exactly what she'd been doing.

For the next couple of minutes, Iain watched the two women lobby statements back and forth as if he wasn't even there. And the longer they volleyed thinly-veiled insults, the clearer things became. Naomi was good friends with the biggest and most widely acclaimed restaurant owner in the Bay Area. One order from him all those months ago and the situation with Whitman's might have been different.

If Iain had been able to secure a massive order right away instead of toiling away for three long months, he wondered if his father's decision might have turned out differently. Instead, it looked as if he'd struggled, and perhaps that was why the company had completely lost faith in his and Maeve's vision. And now he was on the cusp of creating an irreparable divide in his family that couldn't be undone once he set it in motion.

And it could have all been prevented, if only Naomi had cared about him enough to make the introduction.

He rubbed his chest, feeling a hollow ache building as though his heart were collapsing in on itself. *How could she?* He let anger take over from the unpleasant feeling of betrayal. It was easier to be angry than to grieve what he'd lost. What he'd never really had, apparently. As far as Iain was concerned, she could take all her talk of support and understanding and shove it. She might think she didn't trade on her connections, but he'd watched her at the Founders' Ball well before they'd been introduced, and she'd been working the room for her art just as much as he had been for his whiskey.

She was a damn hypocrite.

And he was nothing to her. She'd made that clear the past few days. He was a fool for wanting to come to her aid in the first place. She didn't need him; but what was most evident was she didn't *want* him either.

He slapped his palms to his thighs and pushed to his feet. Looking down at Judith Klein, he forced a smile. "It was great seeing you again, but I really have to run. I have a meeting in about twenty minutes that I can't be late for."

Both women stood, and Mrs. Klein clasped his hand in hers. "Have Naomi give you my number. She might not want to introduce you to Luis, but I have no such rules about leveraging my connections to help a … special friend out." He ignored the slither of discomfort her phrasing gave him in favor of a fresh spurt of anger. Maybe he'd been cozying up to the wrong Klein all along.

Naomi stepped forward. "I'll walk you out."

He stared at her a beat, wondering if she could see the disappointment on his face. "No, don't bother. I know the way."

As he walked out the door, Iain wondered if the last three months—including the time he'd spent holding the dark-haired beauty in his arms—had all just been an epic waste of time.

19

He was leaving. He was *leaving*? Naomi watched Iain stomp out of the room, her stomach sinking. She hadn't thought about what she was doing when he'd said he was outside, only that she wanted nothing more than his strength as a buffer between herself and her family. And now, somehow, her mother had managed to ruin that, too. She drew in a deep breath. She only had a week left before Iain went back to Ireland, and she'd already wasted two days fighting with her family about this ridiculous intervention. So she hadn't come to their stupid events! They'd never come to her gallery openings. Maybe it was about time.

She stood up, trying not to let her eyes keep drifting to the door. He hadn't seemed like he was planning to come back. "Mom, why on earth would you possibly think it's okay for you to insert yourself into my life like this?"

Her mother frowned. "I'm not inserting myself."

Naomi leaned forward. "You have no right to talk to Iain about his whiskey." The words sounded ridiculous even as she said them, and all three of her family members raised their eyebrows.

"May I remind you that I'm the one who signed the contract for his whiskey to be at the Founders' Ball?" Her mother's eyes narrowed. "I have every right to speak to him, both as a vendor and *apparently* as a friend of the family—not that you cared to mention it to us."

"There was nothing to mention," she said through gritted teeth. This was exactly what she'd been hoping to avoid. It was her own stupid fault for bringing him into the house when they were here.

Her brother snorted. "Please. Coming out of a different hotel the morning after the Founders' Ball is one thing. Him showing up in your living room months later is entirely different."

"I'm doing his logo design," she said. It sounded weak, even to her own ears.

"Yeah? How long did that take you? And was that before or after you were in bed with him?"

Naomi had never actually understood the phrase 'seeing red' until now. An actual haze of rage filmed her eyes as she stared at Jacob. "I think you should leave."

"Is he the reason you haven't been returning my calls?" Her mother's lips thinned. "I can't say I approve entirely without knowing more about his family, Naomi. Of course I want you to be happy. But I still don't understand why you wouldn't have sent him to Luis."

"Because I don't want to be like you!" she shouted.

Utter silence fell in the room. Her father and brother exchanged glances, but Naomi had let the floodgates open and now she couldn't stop.

"I don't want to just let all of my dreams die and do absolutely nothing worthwhile unless it's in pursuit of some man's ambitions," she snarled at her mother. "You might be happy living some sort of zombie Stepford Wife life, but it is *not. for. me.* I've told you over and over again, and all you care about is marrying me off to one of your friends' sons! I'm sorry, but fuck that! I have a life, and I have a career, and I am *never* giving it up just so I can change my goddamn last name."

Her mother stared at her. "Is that what you think I did? Is that what you honestly think my life is?" Her expression, as usual, was unreadable, but the fine lines between her brows had deepened with strain.

Naomi threw her hands up helplessly. "I can't see how it could be anything else, Mom."

"Then I suppose we're done here." Her mother rose and left without another word, the front door closing gently behind her.

More silence. Naomi listened to the sound of a car starting in her driveway, then heard the wheels thump onto the street. The sound of the motor faded as she stared at her father and brother.

It was Jacob who finally broke the silence. "That was too far, Nay."

Her anger stirred again. "Says you. Maybe you should go home to your own wife, see what she might have wanted to do with her life."

His lips thinned, and he stood up off of her couch. "I'll be in the car when you're ready, Dad." Another exit, this time with a much louder slam of the door.

Her father sighed. "Naomi—"

"Is it your turn now?" she asked bitterly. "Go for it, Dad. Tell me what an awful person I am for wanting my own life."

He was quiet for a few moments. "You can have your own life and still have other people in it, Naomi. You don't have to be all alone to be successful."

She felt her anger fading into discomfort. "I know that."

"This whiskey man—"

"Iain."

"Iain. You didn't use your connections to help him because you thought it would make you weak?"

She sighed. "Not exactly." Talking about her sex life with her dad was exactly as uncomfortable as she'd always assumed it would be, even though she'd waited until her thirties to do it. "We were just friends. I don't really do commitment, you may have noticed."

His lips tipped into a half smile, and he inclined his head. "I'm a doctor, honey, I'm trained to be observant."

"I just … didn't want people assuming it was more. And if I'd been begging all my friends and relatives to help out a guy, you know perfectly well they'd have started sending out wedding invitations immediately."

Her father pursed his lips. "I think perhaps you're getting a little cynical."

"In my old age?"

"Watch it, now."

"Come on, Dad. Iain walked in the door and Mom was practically demanding to see his income statements and offering to take him ring shopping."

"She wants to see you happy."

"She has no idea what makes me happy."

"I think she's always assumed that what makes her happy are the same things that would do it for you. You're a lot alike, you know."

Naomi stared at her father. "Not. At. All."

He smiled and pushed himself up out of his chair. "Tell you what. Let's take the night to cool off. I'm going to take your mother to that cute restaurant in the town square Noah is always telling me about. Tomorrow, you and she can talk. Just the two of you, no pressure."

She walked him to the door. "What are we suddenly supposed to be talking about?"

He paused in the doorway. "She's here now, honey. Why don't you show her what you do?" He glanced up, in the direction of the studio. She hadn't realized her father even knew about her art, much less where the studio was. He'd always been too busy to acknowledge it. But somebody was keeping him informed, apparently.

"I'll think about it," she said.

---

*N*aomi spent a lonely night tossing and turning in a bed that seemed unnaturally empty without Iain in it, alternately angry with herself, her family, and him. Why hadn't he come back? Why hadn't she swallowed her damned pride and helped him with more than just a good set of logos? Why had her family chosen now, of all possible times, to show up and ruin her life *yet again*?

Her father's words kept ringing in her ears. *You can be*

successful without being alone. He didn't understand, though. He was the successful one, letting her mother spend her entire life supporting him. Raising children, throwing galas, making connections. Naomi shuddered. She couldn't imagine spending her life that way. And she certainly couldn't imagine Iain wanting her to. His pride in her work was evident every time he talked about the branding of Whitman's Revival, and when he asked her curious questions about the sculpture that was nearly finished in her studio upstairs. He hadn't seen it in several days, not since before her family and his had managed to drop bombs in both their lives.

Now maybe he wasn't going to see it at all, because she'd driven him away. She scowled and punched a pillow into a less offending shape. He knew she didn't want her family sniffing around them during the time they had left. His three months were near an end. And with his family dragging him back to Ireland, it wasn't like they were ever going to see each other again anyway. Why was he so angry? He'd done his job. It hadn't been a walk in the park, but he was a good marketer and he'd sold all the whiskey he'd intended to. What would have changed if she'd gotten him a contract with Luis? Judging by what he'd told her about the conversation with his father, his family still wouldn't have had any intention of making the brand a permanent one. *Man, that guy. What a piece of work.* She shook her head. How anybody could treat a man like Iain that way was beyond her.

She sighed and threw off the covers. She wasn't getting any more sleep. And Iain wasn't coming back. Their time together had shrunk to nothing, thanks to her family. Might as well head upstairs and add some final touches to the sculpture, since it was the only thing in her life that seemed to be going right these days.

Predictably, she lost track of time. When her doorbell rang, she blinked out of her reverie and checked the clock. "Shit!" No time to change. She raced down the stairs and opened the door, wincing as her mother's gazed travelled over her dust-covered shirt—Iain's black button-up, as though she could somehow summon him back by wearing it—and loosely-tied hair. "Hi, Mom." She stepped back and let her mother in.

They'd arranged to meet again today, as her father had suggested, but she hadn't intended to look like this. She'd meant to be wearing something casual but nice, something that made her look like an adult woman who had a career, but also friends and an exciting, fulfilling life. Maybe those white linen capris. They screamed 'I've got it all, Mom, stop judging me.' It was the gold buttons on the ankles that did it.

Instead, here she was, letting her impeccable mother into the house looking exactly as she had in high school when she'd first discovered real clay. She'd spent hours at the art studio at school, knowing better than to try to bring her work home. But she'd ruined plenty of clothes back then. Nobody had taught her about industrial laundry cleaners yet. That had come much later.

"Your father says you want to show me something," her mother said as they crossed the hallway.

"I was hoping we could talk a little bit about what I do," Naomi said tentatively. "You've never come to River Hill before, so I've never really been able to show you."

She'd practiced that speech last night, because the first five iterations of it had all included reminders that her parents had also never come to any of her gallery shows, or art openings, or even stopped to look at the sculptures she had on public display at the *library*, for God's sake. She'd managed to narrow it down to this instead.

"I see." Her mother drew in a breath. "I—"

The doorbell rang, and Naomi frowned. She looked at her mother, who was returning the expression. "Were you expecting anybody?"

Naomi shook her head, trying not to let hope slither in. "No." Could it be Iain?

She went back out into the foyer and pulled open the door a little more hastily than she'd intended. She stared blankly at the man who waited on her doorstep.

"I'm here for my son," he snapped.

Her eyes travelled over him as horrified realization began to dawn. He was older, stockier, and grayer, but the Brennan eyes were unmistakable. On Iain, the lines in his cheeks reflected laughter. On this man, they were something else entirely. "You're—"

"Cathal Brennan." He peered past her into the house. "Where the devil is my son?"

"Iain's not here," she said. Her voice sounded squeaky to her own ears.

"Listen, missy, I'm no fool." The old man pointed his finger at her nose. "When two of my children go dark on their family and disappear, I know something's up. And judging by what I've heard since I got here, *you're* to blame."

"Naomi? Who's this?" Her mother had come up behind her.

"Iain's father," she said helplessly. Her mind was whirling.

"Well, how nice. Why don't you come in?" Judith Klein's society face fell into place effortlessly.

Cathal stomped into the house, and Naomi silently shut the door behind him. "I don't understand," she said. "What do you mean, two of your children have disappeared?"

"I haven't heard a drop from Iain since our last call, and Maeve fed her mother some harebrained story about a hen do in Vegas and vanished a couple of days ago. I told you, woman, I'm not an idiot. Maeve's a good girl, she wouldn't do something wild unless Iain talked her into it. And Iain's a family man. A Brennan. He wouldn't insist on staying here unless somebody else talked *him* into it." He glared at her. "I know it was you. Tell me where he is, so I can take him home."

*I*ain's phone buzzed, alerting him to an incoming call. He honestly didn't feel like talking to anyone, but since he was still in the middle of wrapping up the sale of his shares in Brennan's to purchase the distillery down the road, he didn't dare let the call go to voicemail.

Although when he heard the voice on the other end of the line, he wished like hell he had.

"Iain?" He sucked a long breath in through his nose and didn't answer. "I can hear you breathing. I know you're there."

"What do you want, Naomi?" He let all the air out of his lungs on a long gust.

She paused, and he knew his terse response had caught her off guard. Good. She'd blindsided him ten ways to Sunday. It served her right.

"Look," she said, her voice taking on an uncharacteristically nervous tone. "I know things are messed up between us right now—"

He scoffed. "That's one way of putting it."

This time it was Naomi who let out a long sigh. "I'm sorry. Truly. And I plan on telling you exactly how sorry I am, but right now you and I have much bigger fish to fry."

Iain heard rustling in the background, and then raised voices. He recognized the haughty voice of Judith Klein, but he couldn't tell who she was arguing with. The other voice was deep and rumbly and distinctly male. Briefly, he let himself wonder what had gone down after he'd left the other day and whether the Kleins had broken off into factions. From the sound of things, either Naomi's father or brother had decided to come to her defense. He tried not to care. It wasn't his place to think about who Naomi had in her corner now. All he knew was that it wasn't him, and it probably never would be.

When the voices got louder, and he heard the unmistakable sound of Naomi's mom shriek, and then a glass hit the wall, he pushed his pride aside. He might be hurt by the way things had turned about between them, but if the situation was going to turn violent, he didn't want Naomi in that house one second longer. "What's going on over there?"

"That's what I've been trying to tell you," she said, her voice dipping into a whisper. "Your dad showed up looking for you, and—"

"*What?*" He had to have misheard her. There was no way his father was standing in Naomi's house, arguing with her mother, of all people. It was ludicrous. "You're joking."

"I really wish I was," she snapped. He heard a door snick closed behind her, cutting off the argument in the background. "He seems to be operating under the misguided notion that I've convinced you to stay in California."

Fuck. This was not the way he'd planned to tell her he'd be sticking around. He knew they'd have to discuss it at some point, but he'd wanted time to lick his wounds before he had to go back to her and make nice. As upset as he'd been over her betrayal, he'd had some time to think things through, and he knew it wasn't Naomi's fault that his venture with Whitman's hadn't been successful. His father had said it himself: he'd never intended to let Iain and Maeve move forward with their plan. The betrayal from his own family cut deep. Naomi's had put him over the edge.

Still, Iain couldn't help but wonder if he'd gotten the sales he'd needed sooner rather than later—if she'd hooked him up with this Luis fellow months ago when it might have made an impact on his early reports back to Dublin—if he might have been able to change the old man's mind. Now, he'd never know.

And … he was right back to remembering why he was upset with her in the first place.

But as she'd just said, they had bigger fish to fry.

"About that," he said, shoving his hands through his hair and dropping his head back against the padding of the chair he was sitting in. "I'd meant to talk to you about this the other day, but it turns out I'm sticking around River Hill a bit longer than originally thought."

He heard her swallow. "How long?"

He decided to pull off the Band-Aid in one quick tug.

"Permanently, if things go the way Maeve and I are hoping."

"W-w-how?"

"After the bomb my dad dropped on me last week, my sister and I decided to go into business for ourselves. Noah gave us a lead on a distillery that's all kitted out. We're going to make Whitman's here."

"Here?" she croaked.

"Don't worry," he replied, acid churning in his gut. "I don't expect this to change anything between us. I know where I stand."

"Iain …"

Just then a loud thud sounded, and he heard Naomi let out a little shriek. "Shit. It's like World War Three out there. I better go make sure nobody's bleeding."

He heard the door to whatever room she'd been holed up in open. The yelling grew louder and more pronounced. Naomi spoke quickly over the ruckus. "We definitely have a lot to talk about, Iain, but right now we need to keep our parents from literally killing one another."

He opened his mouth to respond, but the line had already gone dead. Shit. Things were really not turning out the way he'd envisioned.

———

This time when he arrived at Naomi's, he didn't bother pussy-footing around. Hearing loud shouts coming from inside, he slammed his car door shut and bounded up the front steps. He turned the handle and let himself in.

And came to an abrupt halt.

Naomi was standing in between his dad and her mom, her hands out as if she was holding each of them back from one another. Iain did a double take. His dad might be an asshole sometimes, but he wasn't a violent man. He'd never seen him raise his voice to a woman, much less turn a mottled shade of red and have spittle flying out the sides of his mouth when doing so. Judith Klein was returning the favor with daggers flying from her eyes with her hands on her hips. Both parents were shouting, leaning past Naomi's restraining hands to accuse each other of all sorts of things.

This was bad. Very, very bad.

When Naomi cast him a grateful glance, her eyes full of apology, it looked like he'd arrived just in time. He took a step into the room, and she let her arms drop to her side, her shoulders hunching in on themselves as she stepped away from him and spoke to his father. "Your son is here."

All at once, his dad quit ranting and turned to face Iain. "You!"

Iain raised an eyebrow. "Me?"

"Yes, you! I've been looking everywhere for you."

He snorted. "Clearly that's not true."

His father took a step forward and raised his hand to tick off items one by one on his fingers as he spat out words. "The bakery, the restaurant, the winery, the bed and breakfast. Each and every one of the people I spoke with said I would find you here. Care to explain yourself?"

Iain planted his feet shoulder width apart and crossed his arms over his chest to give himself a few seconds to absorb that not-so-small nugget of information. He couldn't believe his friends had ratted him out like that. He thought they liked him, that he was one of the gang now, as they were so fond of saying. But friends did not rat other friends out to their parents. He wasn't sure, but he thought it was a bit like Fight Club that way.

His mood was growing darker by the second. And when that happened, he had a tendency to turn into a bit of an asshole—just like his father. He notched his chin in the air defiantly. "No, not particularly."

All at once, Cathal Brennan's bluster evaporated. He sighed and slumped into the nearest chair. "Jesus, Mary, and Joseph," he muttered, shaking his head. "You looked exactly like your mother just then."

The statement didn't come as a surprise to Iain.

While physically he favored his father's side of the family, both he and Maeve had gotten their personality from their mother. So it wasn't much of a shock when his sister had cheerfully joined him to strike out on their own —much as their mother had done once upon a time. More than forty years ago, Colleen O'Brien had left her family behind in Detroit to follow a blue-eyed Brennan back to Ireland, where she'd lived happily ever after since. It was because she was an American citizen—and her children by birth were as well—that any of what Iain had done was possible. Without that dual citizenship, he never would have been able to stay in the U.S. as long as he had, let alone make a serious offer on a piece of commercial real estate

"How is Mom?" he asked, relaxing his stance. It was the one topic he and his father could speak about without raising their voices. Probably because both men loved the woman dearly.

His dad waved his hand. "You know your mam. She'll outlive us all."

Except, she probably wouldn't. His parents weren't getting any younger.

Studying his father intently, Iain realized the vibrant man who'd dominated his life was actually old. His hair was much grayer than it had been at Christmas, and the paunch around his belly was growing more pronounced as the months passed. But most telling of all were the lines bracketing his eyes and mouth. Before, they'd only been evident when his dad scowled—which, admittedly, was frequently—but now they were a permanent fixture on his face. Iain suspected he'd been the cause of many of them.

But Iain had changed, too. Over the last six months, he'd sprouted several gray hairs at his temples that hadn't been there before. The stress of making Whitman's a success rested heavily on his shoulders, and it hadn't been lightened any by the nonstop grief he'd been given by his dad and his brothers along the way.

Which brought him back to the reason for his dad's visit in the first place.

He sighed and dropped down into the chair next to his father. It felt strange to have this conversation in front of Naomi and her mother, who wore identical frowns as they watched—especially considering this was Naomi's house and not really the place for it—but he needed to nip this in the bud once and for all.

"What are you doing here, Dad?"

"John told me you were selling your shares in Brennan's."

Behind him, Naomi gasped, and he turned to look at her over his shoulder. She opened her mouth, no doubt to ask what his dad was talking about, but her mother shushed her before she could get the question out. Judith Klein made a 'go-on' motion with her hands, and Iain dragged his gaze back to his father, briefly wondering just whose side Naomi's mother was on.

He nodded once. "I am. Yes."

His father's eyes turned sad. "Why, son? That's your birthright."

"Right. *My* birthright. Not Maeve's, even though she's more talented than all of us put together."

Cathal let out a weary sigh. "We've been over this before, Iain. This company was built by Brennan *men*."

Iain snorted and crossed his arms over his chest. There was the father he knew. "How very eighteen hundreds of you."

"Yes, that's right." His dad's jaw ticked, and his face grew red. "This business has been in our family since eighteen twenty, and you are the first Brennan to ever try to break it up."

Iain shot out of his chair and paced the perimeter of the room. "Oh, come off it! You know as well as I do the second my shares are available, you're going to pick them up. The only one breaking up this family is you!" He turned to face his father, his chest sawing in and out with anger. "If you had just let Maeve and I do this our way, the way you *promised* we could, none of this would have ever happened. We'd still be two happy Brennan Family Distillers employees. Every single part of us leaving Ireland and buying a distillery here in America is on *you*."

His dad shot Naomi a quick look, and his eyes raked over her bare legs to the tops of her cut off shorts. "Is it because of this one? She's a trifle thin for my liking, but I guess there's no accounting for taste." He snorted and rolled his eyes.

Immediately, Iain saw red. Blood boiling, vein popping, all-his-patience-going-up-in-flames red. "How dare—"

Judith Klein stepped in front of Iain and leaned down to poke his father in the chest. "I don't care what sort of family drama you have going on with your son, but you will *not* speak about my daughter that way. She is more than her looks, which I'll have you know, are absolutely gorgeous. She is a talented, award-winning artist, and your son would be lucky to be with her. No! More than lucky. He should drop to the floor and kiss the feet she walks on!"

Iain turned away so neither of them would see the smile tugging at his lips. This was a very serious moment, but the righteous indignation coming off Mrs. Klein in waves was a sight. He suspected Naomi had never heard so many kind words about herself from her mother. No, he *knew* she hadn't. The startled look on her face confirmed it. She looked like a wee bunny that had been surprised mid-carrot by a stampede of dogs.

Cathal flattened his palm on the tabletop and pushed

to his feet, crowding the elder Klein. "If it weren't for your daughter, my son wouldn't be throwing his future away!"

"Do you not listen? No, of course you don't. You've proven that! He *just* said it was your fault he's moving to America. Not that I'm surprised. An hour with you and I'm ready to relocate to the moon. You insufferable, pig-headed—"

Naomi put her fingers to her mouth and let out an ear-piercing whistle. When their parents fell blessedly silent—Cathal's eyes pinched with distaste, and Judith's jaw hanging open in surprise—Naomi held up her hand. "Enough already."

She turned to Iain's dad. "Personally, I don't give two shits what you think of me, but you've really got it wrong here. Your son—your amazing, intelligent, awesome son —would have worked himself to the bone for your precious family business, if only you'd ever shown him a modicum of respect."

She turned to her mom. "And you! Well, thank you." Her cheeks turned pink, and she glanced away. Iain could tell she was uncomfortable with her mother's praise and wasn't exactly sure how to take it. It was apparent the two women had much to discuss.

As did Iain and his dad. And doing so in front of one another was a recipe for disaster.

He moved to Naomi's side and squeezed her shoulder. "Thank you for calling me. I'm going to grab my dad and head out."

She glanced up at him, her lip trapped between her teeth. "Are you going to be okay?"

Quickly, he stole a glance at his father. His irate, very troublesome father. "Somehow, I'll have to be."

"Call me later and let me know how it goes?"

His eyes flicked between hers. "Is that what you want?"

She nodded, and for a brief second, he thought he saw her eyes begin to shimmer with tears, but then she took a deep breath and nodded. "Yeah. I think we have a lot to talk about."

That was the understatement of the century. "Yeah, I think we do." And he had no idea what the outcome of that conversation would be. Or even what he wanted it to be.

Iain turned to his dad. "Come on. We have a lot to discuss, too."

21

The door closed behind the Brennan men and Naomi blew out a long, slow breath before turning back to her mother. She found Judith Klein watching her closely, with a strange expression on her face.

"What?"

"Naomi …" Her mother's voice sounded almost tentative. "You wouldn't … move to Ireland, would you?"

Naomi stared at her. "I-what?" She felt as though the entire world were spinning around her. Somehow, her feet were stuck to the floor, but she was afraid to move. She might start floating away into the whirlwind that seemed to be hovering over her house.

"Well, you seem to be close with Iain." Her mother's lips twisted. "His father is a piece of work, but children don't always turn out like their parents, as I'm discovering." Her tone was rueful. "You just… I don't want you to leave, Naomi. I'm very proud that you've built your own life, but I'm terrified that you'll realize that you could do it anywhere."

"I spent years living further away than River Hill, Mom. You never said anything." Her stint as a roving artist-in-residence had taken her all over the western half of the United States, living in places that ranged from palatial to bizarre.

"Those were all temporary. I knew you'd come back."

"And you've acted like River Hill is practically Timbuktu ever since I've lived here. You've never visited."

"You've always come home."

"This is still about me not returning your phone calls?"

"Not entirely." Her mother sighed. "I've questioned a lot of your choices over the years, Naomi—" she ignored her daughter's snort of assent "—but I've never, ever, questioned that you love your family. And you know we love you."

"That's true," Naomi said slowly. She *hadn't* ever questioned their love for her. She'd been driven to the point of rage by their attitude toward her, wanted to scream in frustration at them, and made it a point to escape their orbit at every opportunity, but she loved her parents and she knew, deep down in her bones where the knowledge could never be shaken, that they loved her. They just didn't understand her.

"I've always assumed you would eventually fall in love with somebody and settle down, just like I did." Her mother smiled, a secret sort of Mona Lisa half-smile. "I had a fairly wild time in the seventies, you know."

Naomi raised a hand. "I really, really do not want to know."

Her mother shrugged. "Suit yourself. Maybe I'll write a memoir." She paused thoughtfully, her eyes distant. "Might have to wait for a few people to die, though."

"*Mom.*"

"Sorry. We're getting off track. The point is, I assumed you'd settle down with somebody who was… one of us. Somebody we knew, whose family we knew, whose future we understood."

"All evidence to the contrary?"

"Yes. Some assumptions you just can't shake."

"And now?"

"Is he really staying here?" Her mother frowned. "His father seems very certain he'll go back to Ireland."

Naomi felt her heart cracking again. How could there be any pieces left to break? "I don't know. We haven't spoken about it." They hadn't spoken about *anything*. Apparently, he and his sister had come up with some sort of plan to stay in California, and put it into action, but the need-to-know crowd hadn't included her. She couldn't put into words how much that hurt, especially not to her mother. Even if her mother, of all people, suddenly seemed so sympathetic.

"Well, I'm sure we'll find out eventually." Judith patted her daughter's arm. "I want to hear about your work."

"You do?" Naomi swallowed the lump in her throat.

"Didn't you hear me telling that obnoxious Irishman how amazing it is? Next time I yell at him, I want to come armed with more than a mother's intuition."

Naomi giggled through a wave of emotions that threatened to swamp her. Pride, relief, grief, heartbreak, and a little bit of awe. She knew that her mother had the ability to annoy the stuffing out of *her*, but who knew she was able to turn that ability on for perfect strangers? She'd practically given Cathal Brennan an aneurysm. One he fully deserved, in Naomi's opinion.

"Come on. Let's start with the design work that pays the bills, and then I'll show you the studio where all the fun stuff happens."

As her mother paged through her portfolio, which now included both Max's menu design and Iain's whiskey branding package, Naomi's fingers drifted to the phone in her pocket. Should she text him? What would she say?

Sorry my mom turned your dad into a raving lunatic?

Are you still leaving?

What are you and your sister planning?

Is everything okay?

Please stay?

She shook her head and pulled her hand away from her phone. He'd made it clear that he and his dad had a lot to talk about. And she had her own life. Her family was worried about her. And she'd woken up this morning to an email from Z Gallery letting her know that the space was ready for her to set up her show. She had more than enough going on without worrying about Iain's plans, whatever they were. If he didn't see fit to include her … well, it was only what they'd agreed on in the beginning.

"This is the restaurant your father took me to last night." Her mother tapped the page she was looking at. "I like what you did to freshen the design here."

"Thank you." Naomi leaned over her mother's shoulder and pointed. "I thought reorganizing the sections was pretty effective, and removing all the ridiculous frames and curlicues in favor of just a few basic typographic ornaments really brings out the simplicity that Max goes for."

"You know the owner well?"

"He's a friend."

Her mother pursed her lips, and Naomi watched her, mesmerized by the faint facial cues that indicated that Judith Klein's mind was working, making connections and sorting facts. All she said, though, was, "The food was delicious."

"He was nominated for a James Beard award a couple of years ago."

"Hmm. Well deserved, I'm sure."

"I'll let him know you approve."

Her mother smiled. "I'm sure I can get in touch with him myself."

Naomi narrowed her eyes. "What are you planning, Mom?"

Her mother raised her hands defensively. "Nothing! Just thinking of how charming this little town you've settled in is, and how entrepreneurial all your friends seem to be."

Well, that was certainly true. River Hill thrived on food and wine, and Naomi had somehow found herself in the thick of a group of small business owners who formed the current backbone of the town's economy. Angelica had once told her she thought Noah had formed his group of friends based solely on how they could help each other out on dates with food and drinks, and she'd laughed at the kernel of truth in it. Naomi had been along for the ride, but she'd drunk her fair share of Noah's wine, eaten

Max's food, and feasted on Sean's baking enough to make her daily yoga sessions a necessity for more than just her peace of mind.

"They're all good people. I'm really happy here."

"I know a few people in the food industry, you know. I think they'd be very interested in your friend."

Naomi rolled her eyes. "You just can't help yourself, can you?"

"Naomi, what's the point in having a wide circle of friends and acquaintances if you can't introduce them to each other? People like meeting other people. It's human nature."

"Whatever, Mom. Just … maybe *ask* Max before you interfere in his life?"

Her mother sniffed. "Fine. Now, where's this studio?"

"Upstairs." She led her mother to the stairs, explaining how she'd renovated the place. "Jacob said I hurt the resale value."

They reached the door at the top of the stairs, and Naomi opened it to reveal the true home of her heart. Her mother's eyes widened. "Your brother was wrong, dear."

Naomi grinned. "Glad to hear it." Her mother might be many things, but she was absolutely reliable when it came to real estate and home design.

"This is my most recent work." She gestured at the finished sculpture on the table.

She'd glazed and fired the piece yesterday, and it now sat proudly in the center of her studio, waiting to be packed into a crate sitting open on the floor next to the table. Ready for transport to the gallery, to be revealed to everyone who walked in the door and anybody who might click on the website. This was certainly going to be the featured piece of her show. It was her finest sculpture ever, and every time she looked at it she wanted to weep.

The lump of clay she'd sat on her workbench weeks ago was now an incredibly lifelike human heart, striated with raised veins and surrounded by a mesh formed by the interwoven fingers of two hands clutching it carefully. Between the fingers of the hands sprouted delicate strands of a plant that strongly resembled Irish barley, the braided fronds gently edging the caging fingers aside to reveal the heart within. She hadn't realized what she was doing until she was done. She stared at it, lips thin, and heard her mother gasp.

"Naomi, it's beautiful."

"Thank you."

Judith Klein traced the strands of barley that were freeing the caged heart with one gentle finger, and then looked up at her daughter. "Has he seen it?" No need to ask which *he* she meant.

Naomi shook her head.

"Are you going to show it to him?"

"Probably not."

"Naomi—"

"What good would it do, Mom? This was never meant to be permanent. I don't do relationships, remember?"

"People change, Naomi." Her mother glanced over at the sculpture. "Given the right incentive."

"It doesn't matter. He's leaving."

"Leaving the country, or leaving you?"

"Is there a difference?"

"Ireland isn't that far," her mother said. "Lots to do there."

"Do I seem like the sort of woman who would chase a man across an ocean?"

Her mother looked her up and down, then smiled slowly. "No. My daughter is the sort of woman men cross an ocean to find."

Naomi felt tears welling up. Again. "Thanks, Mom."

"Well, if he can't recognize how wonderful you are, it's his problem," her mother said firmly.

Naomi sighed. "He's been great, Mom. I'm the one who screwed it up. I freaked out about the idea of using my personal connections to help him, and I didn't even talk to him about it."

"Why?"

"Honestly, at this point, I don't even know." She shook her head. "I feel like an idiot. Do you know, if we hadn't been sleeping together, I wouldn't have thought twice about calling Luis for him?"

Her mother's eyebrows shot up. "The sex made a difference? Must have been good sex."

"Mom. I am *not* taking this conversation in that direction."

Her mother shrugged. "Your loss. I told you I had a lot of fun in the seventies."

"Ew."

"So, why didn't you help him?"

"Because I knew Luis would tell you, and then it would be like when you shoved me into Andy Weinstein's car when I was seventeen."

"I never shoved you."

"Mom, you literally closed the door on my foot."

"Well, you were late."

"Because I didn't want to go, and you were so blinded by the idea of me magically falling in love with Doctor Weinstein's son that you didn't care about what I wanted. And you made sure nobody else did, either. All I heard about for weeks was what a cute couple we were, and how everyone was looking forward to our wedding. I was *seventeen!*"

Her mother winced. "I suppose our friends can be overly enthusiastic sometimes."

"Do you remember in college, when Ross Jacobs gave me that cute little rose gold ring he'd gotten on his trip to Montana? We weren't dating, just friends, and he thought of me when he saw it because it looked like a sculpture I was working on. And then, when I was home on break, Mrs. Greene stopped me in the cereal aisle in the grocery store to wiggle her eyebrows at me and ask about the 'special ring' I'd gotten from a man."

"I … may have mentioned it to a few people."

"Can you at least try to imagine how uncomfortable that made me feel?"

Her mother nodded. "I'm sorry."

Naomi shook her head. "Iain and I were just having a good time together. I didn't need all of San Francisco society Googling him to see if he was good enough for me."

Her mother was silent, staring at the sculpture.

"What are you thinking?"

"I'm thinking that he's been very good for you," her mother said. "But also that I want to see that piece in the gallery, along with everything else. I'm amazed by what you do, Naomi."

She stepped closer and slung her arm around her mother's shoulders in a one-armed hug. "I don't think I've ever told you, but I'm pretty sure I got all of my artistic skill from you."

Her mother flushed, then smiled. "Well, your father can't even draw a stick figure when he tries, so it had to come from somewhere."

"I mean it. You have amazing taste, Mom. It just came out a little differently in me."

"Well, I'm proud of the way you use it," her mother said, returning the hug.

"Thanks. And Mom—thanks for coming. Thanks for worrying about me."

"Try and stop me," her mother said. "What's next?"

Naomi stepped away and filled her lungs with air, trying to ignore the pinch in her chest that felt like heartbreak. It was time to move on. Her next move had been planned from the beginning, and she was ready to make it. "Next, I head to the gallery in San Francisco to set up the show. It's time to pack up and leave River Hill for awhile."

22

*I*ain and his father had spent the last forty-five minutes going round and round with one another, only to reach the same exact point they'd started: Iain intended to stay put in River Hill, and Cathal Brennan didn't want to let it happen. Now, they sat across from one another in awkward, stony silence while they waited for the conference call to connect with the rest of the Brennans back in Ireland.

Iain had texted an SOS to Maeve thirty minutes before, but his sister still hadn't responded. While that was very much in keeping with her personality, now was not the time for her to be indulging in one of her famous silences. He really needed her by his side, presenting a united front on their endeavor.

"What's this about you selling your shares?" Fionn demanded without so much as a hello the moment the call connected. Next to him was Braden, wearing a sour grimace, and to Iain's surprise, their mother. He tried to read her expression for some indication of where she fell on the matter, but Colleen Brennan had the finest poker face in six counties.

He dragged his eyes away from her and stared straight into the camera. "Maeve and I are buying a distillery here, and I need the capital for the deal to go through." He needed them to understand that his mind was made up and there would be no swaying him from this path.

According to the family lawyer, no one could actually block the sales of his shares. His father and brothers knew that too, so the only move they had left was to try and persuade him not to. But persuasion had never been their strong suit. Most of the Brennan men operated more on the bully end of the spectrum.

Knowing his brothers as he did, Iain had already anticipated every point against his plan they could toss his way during this conversation. Opening their own distillery wouldn't be easy, but Iain was confident he and Maeve could make it successful. After all, there were several other small, artisan outfits operating at a profit all over the U.S. And none of them had the pedigree he and Maeve brought to the table.

Braden leaned in and sneered at the screen. "You've had some stupid ideas—"

Iain rolled his eyes and leaned back in a gesture of nonchalance. He was not going to let Braden rile him up. Cutting his older brother off before he could say something that'd make him look like even more of an ass, Iain said, "If you're trying to sweet talk me into compliance, you're doing a—"

"Sorry I'm late!" Maeve called out, rushing in through

the door. "The bank took forever." She plopped down on the sofa next to Iain. "What did I miss?"

Iain did a double-take. "The bank?"

Maeve glanced between him, their father, and the laptop screen. "Ah," she mused. Everyone but she and the Brennan family matriarch wore matching looks of confusion. "I guess you hadn't gotten to that part yet."

"What part?" their father barked, glaring at his daughter.

Maeve chewed her lip and shot Iain a look he couldn't quite interpret. If it were anyone else, he might think that was guilt darkening her expression, but he knew his sister better than that. There wasn't an underhanded bone in her body.

But it wasn't Maeve who answered. To Iain's surprise, his mother cleared her throat. "The part where I announce I'm going into business with Iain and Maeve. I funded the distillery."

"You *what*?!" Fionn and Braden cried in unison.

And all at once, the two rooms, one on each side of the ocean, both erupted into a wild cacophony of competing voices and gestures.

Eventually, when it became clear no one was going to cede the floor, Iain marched over to the sink and pulled out the bullhorn he'd found in the cupboard underneath it several days ago. He had no clue why Max was keeping it under there, but he wasn't going to question the man when it was the perfect way to get everyone to shut up and listen to their mother.

He flicked on the switch and raised it to his mouth.

"Hey!" he shouted, his voice echoing loudly in the tiny room.

Maeve winced and leaned away while his father covered his ears with both hands.

"What the hell was that for?" Cathal shouted back at his son.

Iain dropped the bullhorn to his side and returned to the couch. He made a dramatic show of setting it down on the cushion next to him, so everyone would know he'd use it again if they got out of hand. He turned back to the screen. "You were saying, Mom?"

She smiled at Iain, and for the first time all afternoon, he thought everything might be okay. "I was saying that I'm investing in your distillery." Iain glanced at Maeve. Her mouth was split in a devious grin. He'd forgotten how much she looked like their mother, but with the both of them looking like cats who'd just stolen a distillery's worth of cream, the resemblance was clear.

"For almost two hundred years," Colleen O'Brien Brennan continued firmly, "the men of this family have made *other* men richer, while the women have been kept out. At no point have any of *you*—" she cast a pointed look at each of the men of her family "—sought to rectify that."

Iain's father crossed his arms over his chest and scowled, his chin jutting out defensively. "I love you dearly, Colly, but you know as well as I do that tradition matters. Especially in a company like ours." They'd clearly had this conversation before.

"Yes, I do know that. But everyone on this call *also* knows that you boys have benefited tremendously from it too, while women like Maeve have been harmed by it." She looked at Iain. "Son, in your professional opinion, would Brennan's have taken any flack for making Maeve a shareholder?"

It took Iain a moment to respond. Frankly, he was still in shock. He'd known his mom had a strong feminist streak in her, but he'd never seen her publicly countermand his father, much less state an opposing position about the patriarchal nature of the company's founding or the way it continued to be run. From the sound of things, however, this wasn't the first time she'd brought it up with his father. Now, he wondered what other changes she'd been silently working for behind the scenes for all these years. And he couldn't help but appreciate her pointed reference to his own professional qualifications with her question.

He shook his head. "Maybe twenty years ago, but not now."

Braden scoffed.

"I'm serious," Iain continued. "Whether you want to acknowledge it or not, times are changing. There are women distillers now, famous ones. And female brewmasters who are making a *killing* in the field. If we'd put Maeve at the forefront of our operations years ago, we would have been trailblazers. Instead, we've stagnated and lost ground with younger buyers. We look like a company run by old men, for old men. And newsflash—those old men are dying off. We need new customers."

His father's eyes flashed with fury. "If it were up to you, you'd kill off everything that makes Brennan's *Brennan's*. You have no sense of duty or honor!"

Iain's belly clenched with hurt. Nothing his father said

was true, but he knew there was nothing he could ever do to make the old man see the situation any differently. All Iain had ever tried to do was keep Brennan's at the forefront of Irish whiskey. He'd given everything to the company that bore his family name … right up until the moment it became apparent their loyalty didn't extend back to him. Or his sister. "Then I guess the only thing that's left to say is I'm sorry you feel that way." He turned to his mom. "Thank you, Mom. I appreciate what you're doing."

Iain pushed off the sofa and set his hand on Maeve's shoulder. She looked up at him with eyes that glittered with unshed tears. She might be willing to rebel with him, but she hated true conflict. It couldn't be helped, though. He gave her hair a soft tug. "I can't be here anymore. Bring me up to speed later?"

She nodded as Iain stepped around her … and straight out the door.

Iain lost track of how long he'd been sitting in the gazebo in the middle of the town square, but his untouched coffee had long since turned cold, and the sun had set some time ago. He flipped his phone over and over in his hands, debating whether or not he should call Naomi. That had been his first inclination, but with the way things were between them, he didn't know if that was the best course of action. When he'd left her place earlier that afternoon, they'd said they would talk. But about what? He'd been paralyzed by wondering about the answer to that question for what felt like hours.

The decision was taken out of his hands when a lone figure strolled across the grass, up the steps of the gazebo, and stopped in front of him. He leaned back and looked up at the only woman who'd ever had the ability to tie him up in knots. "Hey."

"Hey yourself." She nodded to the space next to him. "Mind if I sit down?"

"Sure." He scooted over to make room on the bench for the both of them.

When she sat, he turned to face her and took a deep breath before speaking. He had so many conflicting emotions running through him, and there were so many things he knew they needed to discuss. "Naomi, I—"

"Iain, I—" She smiled, her lips forming a thin line on her beautiful face and gestured for him to go first.

"How'd you find me?"

"Technically, I didn't. Your sister called Max wondering if he knew where you might be. He called Noah, who called me. I was on my way out of town but had stopped for coffee." She held up her to-go cup with The Hollow Bean's black and white logo front and center. "I was walking back to my car when I had this strange urge to cut across the square. I looked up, and there you were. Like serendipity." She bumped her shoulder against his, and it brought a smile to his face. Maybe the first real one he'd felt all day.

Iain knew he should explain to Naomi why Maeve was looking for him, or why he hadn't answered Max's phone call or Noah's text message, but he could only focus on one thing. "You said something about heading out of town?" She was *leaving?*

Naomi took a long sip of her coffee, her eyes finding his over the rim of the cup. Iain couldn't say why, but he got the sense that she was stalling. Eventually, she swallowed and nodded. "Yes. I need to get down to the gallery and get all my work set up for the show next week."

Iain felt a quick stabbing pain in his chest … exactly like the one he'd felt when they'd been driving home from Gavin's show all those weeks ago. At the time, he'd thought it was indigestion. But now he knew better. It was love. And heartbreak. And it fucking sucked.

He was happy for Naomi's success—honestly—but he was a bit sad, too. Everything between them had fallen apart so quickly. Iain realized he'd taken it for granted that he'd get to see the final pieces she'd chosen for her exhibition because he'd be at her house helping her pack them up. Instead, he had no clue how her headline piece had turned out. Or what it even was. It seemed as though he didn't have a clue about a lot of things where she was concerned.

Attempting to mask the riot of emotions running through him, he pulled his eyes from hers and looked out over the square. "You finished the sculpture, then?"

"I did. It's …" Naomi trailed off and let out a long sigh. "It's more than I ever thought it could be. It's also not exactly what I thought it was going to be, either."

He turned back toward Naomi and studied her face. She didn't look unhappy, but he knew her, and while she might not have said the words, her voice had revealed some sort of inner struggle with the finished piece. Almost as if she knew it was good, but she wasn't sure she actually liked it.

"I'm sure it's beautiful," he told her. Because everything she touched was beautiful. Even if it wasn't lasting.

Her eyes turned hazy for a brief second—as if she was suddenly lost in thought—and then she blinked, and the look was gone. "Enough about me, though. Noah wanted me to make sure that I let you know that your dad had left."

"Left?"

She nodded. "Yeah, apparently he's on his way to the airport now."

Iain blew out a breath. "Wow. That's …" He didn't know what it was. At any rate, he didn't think it was a good thing. Not much shot at closure on the family feud, anyway.

Naomi laid a hand on his knee. "I'm sorry things didn't go the way you wanted with your family."

Iain's gaze dropped to her hand and then back up. Misinterpreting his look, she pulled it away, and he felt the loss of contact deep in his bones. "Thanks. I can't say that I'm surprised, but I really hoped we could work something out."

Just then his phone buzzed in his hand. He flipped it over to see it was Maeve.

Naomi stood. "I should really get going. And you should go talk with your sister." She nodded toward his phone, Maeve's name glowing in large print over the green 'answer' button.

Iain nodded and stood, shoving the device into his

pocket. Maeve could wait a few minutes more. As if compelled by some invisible force, he took a step forward. And then another. Naomi was his sun, and he was helpless to fight her gravitational pull. Wherever she was, he wanted to be too. "Yeah, and you should get on the road." Without conscious thought, he raised his hand and pushed a lock of her hair behind her ear, dragging the tip of his finger down her neck until he felt her skin pebble beneath his touch. "Drive safe."

"I will." With her eyes locked on his, she bit her lip … and then looked away. "We'll talk soon."

He nodded, and then realized she might not be able to see him in her peripheral vision. "Yeah, call me and let me know how the show goes." He took a step back and shoved his hands in the pockets of his coat.

Naomi gave him a small nod and then turned on her heel and strode quickly out of the gazebo. Iain just stood there, watching her go, wondering if he'd ever get the chance to watch her walking toward him. Toward *them*.

He let his shoulders slump as he turned to leave, too. He pulled his phone back out of his pocket and hit the 'call back' button waiting on the screen. "Hey sis, what's up?"

As he walked from the town square back to his apartment, Iain listened with increasing astonishment as his sister explained that after he'd left their mother had laid into their brothers and father. By the time the smoke had cleared, Cathal Brennan was crawling back to Ireland with his tail between his legs to beg for his wife's forgiveness. The way Maeve told it, he'd be begging for Iain's next—all from the safety of a different continent.

After all he'd gone through, Iain no longer had to sell his shares of Brennan Family Distillers if he didn't want to. No matter what he decided, though, their mother wanted to use the money she'd inherited from her own father to get the distillery up and running. For generations, she'd said, Brennan men had been investing in their sons; it was time an O'Brien invested in her daughter. He and Maeve could either take the money as a loan, or she could stay on as a silent investor—whatever Maeve and Iain wanted was what Colleen Brennan wanted for them.

By the time Iain had hung up with his sister, his mind was reeling. He'd never expected their mother to defy their father in such spectacular fashion. Then again, he'd never expected his father to betray him so spectacularly either. According to Maeve, an apology would be forthcoming, but at the moment, Iain didn't know if he was ready to accept. The hurt was still too fresh.

As he lumbered up the narrow steps to his tiny place, his feet dragging after the emotionally taxing day he'd just had, he thought long and hard about exactly what it was that he wanted.

He wanted Maeve to have her distillery, and he wanted to be the one to run it.

But most of all, he wanted a certain recalcitrant artist by his side through it all. Now, he just had to convince her that's where she belonged.

23

"Thanks, Jim," Naomi called as the gallery owner left her in the space with a wave. He'd let her in, helped her carry the heaviest crates, and showed her where he kept the hanging supplies in the back room. Now he was off to a meeting, or lunch, or whatever it was gallery owners did when they weren't actively hosting shows. He'd left her here alone to set up, with a key to the front door to lock up when she was finished.

Alone was the key word, she reflected as she examined the gallery space. Empty blank walls and the sturdy white columns of display tables waiting for her art stared back at her. She ought to be thrilled that she was here. She'd given Iain the message about his father and had managed to escape before either of them had gotten clingy or weird about a relationship that was clearly over.

So why did it feel like she was running away? She'd been planning this show since the night she met Iain; she'd known she would be driving out to the city today. She'd checked in to a hotel near the gallery, ready to stay for the weeklong duration of her show. Opening night was tomorrow night. She'd be here. Iain would be… well, apparently, he'd be in River Hill, setting up a new distillery. Unless that last conversation had gone differently, and his father had left because Iain was expected to follow him back to Ireland shortly.

She couldn't dwell on it. They'd agreed. Three months, then part as friends. They hadn't managed the parting as friends part as well as she could have hoped, but they were certainly parting. Iain was moving on, working with his sister. She was moving on, too. Z Gallery was a huge win for her—Jim's clientele were rich, and most of them had both residential and commercial spaces they liked to fill with art like hers. He'd told her when she arrived that he fully expected to sell every single piece she'd brought. When she'd opened the crate that contained her heart sculpture, he'd sucked in a startled breath and then looked up at her with an expression of pure glee on his face.

"You know how in cartoons, people's eyes turn into dollar signs?" He'd pointed to his own brown eyes, nearly hidden behind thick-framed black hipster glasses. "Mine are doing that right now."

She'd laughed, but it had hurt to breathe. Now, she lifted the piece carefully out of the crate, gently brushing the fragments of packing material away. She set it on the stand waiting on the central pedestal, a basic, squat white column that was set directly in the center of the gallery. Several of the lights that hung on roving tracks throughout the ceiling had been aimed at it, so the column was bathed in plenty of warm light. It was set up exactly as she'd requested, and this piece would shine as the central focus of the show. It was the culmination of months of work. Years, if you considered the journey she'd traveled in life to get to the point where she was capable of producing something so thoroughly emotive.

And as she stared at it, she felt a gnawing sensation in her stomach and a horribly strong urge to hide it away so that nobody could see it. She didn't *want* to sell it. The idea of some random guy in a suit putting her *actual heart* on display in his condo made her ill. She'd reached for the little stack of cards intended for sale notifications twice now, the urge to write NOT FOR SALE on one of them getting stronger and stronger.

She shook her head again. She was getting maudlin. She needed to pull herself together. Taking long, slow breaths, she turned slowly around in a circle, examining her work. She'd taken each of the pieces Jim had requested out of their protective packaging and placed them carefully on their stands. The printed cards that bore her name, logo, and brief artist statements for each piece had already been slipped into the waiting plexiglass holders attached to each display. She was nearly done. All that was left was the final *zhuzh*, as her mother would say. The last little fidgets and moving of things an inch to the left here, half an inch to the right there that would make the set up truly perfect.

She pulled out her phone to check the time and bit her lip.

For the first time in her life, she *didn't want to be here.*

She winced. She'd spent her entire career working toward this moment. But all she could think about was whether Iain was going to be leaving. If he was going back to Ireland or staying in River Hill. If he was going to work full-time on the new whiskey. If he wanted to see her again.

Because she definitely wanted to see him. It was time to stop fooling herself. She was crazy in love with her Irish whiskey man, and every minute she spent here fiddling with her sculptures was another minute she was losing on the road back to River Hill to ask him if he felt the same. She'd done what she'd needed to do here, and she could easily make it back in time to do even more tomorrow morning if she needed to. She closed the crate that had held her heart piece and carried it back into the storage room that was hidden from view by a whitewashed wall. Emerging back into the gallery, she looked around at her work, glowing dimly in the warmth of the carefully-positioned lights. She let professional satisfaction wash over her once more. She'd done it. She turned her gaze toward the door.

The entire glass storefront of the gallery had been covered in a vinyl wrap advertising her show; it served the dual purpose of generating advertising buzz and hiding the inside of the gallery until the show was completely set up inside. It was one of Jim's special tricks that made Z Gallery so popular. She'd long since shaken off most of the imposter syndrome that had plagued her first few years as a professional artist but seeing her own giant face and stylized signature taking up an entire window had definitely given her pause when she'd arrived.

Now, she hurried to the covered door and wrenched it open, juggling the key Jim had given her with her own car keys. She stepped out into the bright sunlight, shading her eyes against the change from the darkened gallery, and immediately collided with a solid body.

"What—" She felt arms go around either side of her to catch her, and familiar hands at her waist. "Iain? What? How—"

"Hi." It was really him. That low, smooth voice couldn't be anyone else, not that she'd needed the proof with the warmth of his steadying touch infusing her body with a feeling that only Iain seemed able to bring about. Every time he touched her, she was reminded how much she wanted him.

Her eyes had finally adjusted to the light, but he still seemed to have a halo shining around his head. Probably her imagination. Or maybe he was just that good. "I'm so glad to see you," she said.

He quirked an eyebrow and lifted his lips into a half-smile. "Are you?"

"Yes! Oh—" She tugged him back through the door. "Come in here, I'm being blinded. I was just coming to see you." She blurted it out as though it wasn't something she'd been agonizing over practically since she'd arrived at the gallery. As if it made all the sense in the world. Maybe because it did.

Iain hadn't quite let go of her yet, his hands still lingering at her hips. "You were?"

She nodded. "I shouldn't have left so quickly."

"You had a show to prepare," he said, shrugging. "Speaking of which—" He looked around, brows going higher as he took in the nearly-finished setup. "This is great, Naomi."

"Thanks," she said.

His gaze returned to her. "This is the real deal for you, isn't it? The big time?"

She nodded. "There's still a lot on my bucket list as an artist, but this is a huge step. It'll get my foot in a lot of doors. Especially …" she stopped, feeling her heart start to race. He hadn't seen it yet. Her body was blocking his view of the central space. She stepped aside. "Especially when they see this."

She watched his face as he examined the final version of the sculpture she'd been creating the entire time they'd been together. It was practically an artistic record of their relationship. And it said exactly what she'd been trying to figure out how to say for the last several hours. Days, even. *She loved him.* She loved him, and he'd made her a better person.

His eyes widened and he moved closer to the sculpture. His hand seemed to move of its own volition, reaching out toward the large clasped hands surrounding the heart, tracing the lines of Irish barley nudging the clay fingers aside. "Naomi…"

She swallowed. "Do you like it?" Her voice wobbled a little on the last word, and she winced. She was already feeling vulnerable enough. No need to rub it in.

"It's incredible," he whispered. He touched the vein-striated heart emerging from its cage, then turned to her, his eyes full of some unreadable emotion. "Don't sell it." His voice was low, and hard. "Please."

She swallowed. And nodded. "I was already thinking about telling the gallery owner it's spoken for."

His smile was slow, but it felt like dawn breaking over

the Pacific when it washed over her. "Actually, I know the perfect place for it."

"You do?"

He reached out and took her hand, then twined their fingers together just like the barley twined through the fingers of the sculpture. "Our tasting room."

"Your what?" The last she'd heard, his father was storming off to Ireland, and he and his sister were about to either go rogue with a distillery of their own or go crawling back to the family, and neither scenario had included enough money to furnish a full tasting room.

He pulled her closer to him, until their bodies were touching. She rested her head on his shoulder. "As it happens, my mother saved the day."

"Mothers are strange that way," she murmured, remembering her most recent conversation with her own mother. Judith Klein intended to be front and center during the gallery's opening. And she'd even promised not to tell any of her friends about it. She was just going to be there, to support her daughter without interfering. "What did yours do?"

"She gave Maeve the money to buy the distillery. All of it."

Naomi's head popped off of Iain's shoulder and she stared at him. "You're kidding."

He shook his head. "She also did a number on my father and brothers. I got the most astonishing phone call from my dad this morning. He *apologized* to me."

"I need to meet your mother," Naomi said without thinking.

"About that..."

She gulped. "That is … I mean … I didn't…" She struggled mightily to say what was in her heart. After all, it was the first time she'd ever felt this way, much less told someone else.

He held up a hand. "I'm going to say it first. I need to, I think." He took a deep breath. "I love you, Naomi Klein. I love that you're complicated, and I love that you're loyal, and I love literally every single thing you do in bed, let's not forget that part. I also love that you've made my life immeasurably better since you came into it, and I don't want you out of it. Ever."

She swallowed. "I love you too." It came out as a whisper, and he grinned.

"I'm going to need you to say that a little louder, my darling commitment-phobe."

She laughed. "I love you too, Iain Brennan. That sculpture is *my* heart. You've pulled it out from where I was hiding it. I was keeping it caged away because I was so scared of what other people would do if they saw me using it, I think. My family, their friends, even my own friends. But you've let me live life with love, and friendship, and I never want to go back."

"So…" He paused. "What do we do now?"

She slid her arms around his neck and let her lips linger near his. "I can think of a few things. But you're going to have to back away from the art."

His hands lingered over her ass. "I'm staying in River Hill, you know."

"Permanently?"

He nodded. "We've signed the contract for the distillery. I still have my shares of Brennan's, and I'll probably do some consulting for them on the marketing side once in a while to keep my face in front of the European movers and shakers, but Maeve and I are all in here."

"Do you think you might be looking for a more permanent place to live?"

The little lines in between his eyebrows crinkled as he frowned. "I… suppose?" He searched her face, as if he were unsure of where she was going.

But she'd never been surer of anything in her life. "Do you want to move in with me?"

He dropped his lips to hers in answer as he deftly backed away from the art.

Thank you for reading THE DISTILLER'S DARLING. If you loved Naomi and Iain as much as we do, please consider leaving a review wherever you purchased this e-book. Reviews are a great way for other readers to discover books they may enjoy too!

UP NEXT: THE BAKER'S BEAUTY

THE BAKER'S BEAUTY
(River Hill #3)

After tragedy struck, Sean Amory left L.A. to come home to River Hill to work at his family's bakery. The familiar surroundings soothe his raw nerves while the gorgeous brunette who jogs past every morning has another effect entirely. And when she helps him out of a bind, he learns Jess is even sweeter than the apple fritters he's become famous all over town for.

Former beauty queen Jessica Casillas-Moore hasn't eaten carbs since she was fourteen, but that doesn't stop her from jogging past The Breadery every morning. And when she meets the handsome baker who works there, Sean is every bit as mouthwatering as the pastries he serves. And so much better for her waistline.

But between her family's disapproval and his haunting

past, the odds seem stacked against them. Can Sean and Jess learn to trust in each other and their growing love, or is their relationship a recipe for disaster?

Chapter One

"I don't know much about interventions, but I think you're doing it wrong." Sean Amory peered over the rim of his glass at his friends. "For starters, I'm pretty sure you're not supposed to do it at a bar."

Max Vergaras rested his elbow on the sticky surface of The Hut's bar top, making a face as his shirt moved in a different direction than his skin. "It's the only place we can find you these days."

"It's here or work," Noah Bradstone added, taking a seat on the other side of Sean as Iain Brennan nodded in agreement from behind him.

"So?" Sean sipped his whiskey, ignoring the concern written all over their faces. "Disappointed I'm not drinking yours?" He aimed the barb at Iain.

"We don't distribute here. Just Frankie's," the Irishman answered with an easy shrug.

"I don't drink at Frankie's."

"Not anymore, you don't," Max said. He owned Frankie's, and when he wasn't in the kitchen, he was behind the bar. He had a fair idea of how much his customers drank on any given night, which was precisely why Sean had stopped drinking there.

"I didn't know you were hurting for business."

Max rolled his eyes but didn't bother to respond. Frankie's—and many of the other businesses that rounded out River Hill's ridiculously charming downtown—had never been better. Some recent high profile publicity for the town had brought the tourists in droves, and everyone appreciated the extra income, if not the actual vacationers.

Noah leaned in. "Sean, you know why we're here."

"Slumming?" Noah's highbrow wine labels weren't available at The Hut any more than Iain's fancy whiskey was.

"You need help." Noah's thick eyebrows snapped down into a frown. "Seriously."

"I'm fine."

"You're drinking too much."

"Maybe you're not drinking enough." These men had been his friends for years. Iain was new to the pack, having moved to River Hill to cohabit with the notoriously prickly Naomi Klein last year, but the others knew him well. Right now, though, Sean wished he'd never met them.

"Listen." Noah was taking the lead again. Sean briefly imagined slamming his friend's head into the ancient bar top in front of them, then shook his head slightly to clear it. Violence wasn't his style. Did the guys have a point? He transferred his glare from the group to the glass in front of him as Noah continued speaking. "My therapist is always saying to think about what it would *look* like if you confronted the things you're running from, if your worst fears came true. Then—"

Sean snorted a bitter laugh. "That's the last thing I need to imagine."

He knew *exactly* what it would look like. Cal Grissom's too-pale face, slack in death, had been floating into his vision every time he closed his eyes for the last year and a half. Drinking was the only thing that blurred the grisly image, the only thing that stopped him waking up in the middle of the night reaching helplessly toward the kid's hand, dangling loosely over the side of the perfectly made-up hotel room bed, still clutching the pill bottle that had killed him. Rigor mortis had made his fingers curve to the shape of the bottle even after they'd pried it out, a detail Sean wished every single day he could forget.

"I think you should call a therapist. If not mine, then a different one." Noah reached out and plucked the half-empty glass from Sean's loose grip. "This isn't cutting it, my friend." He sniffed the glass. "I'm pretty sure Johnnie Walker's degree is strictly honorary."

"Fuck you." He'd meant for the insult to be biting, but it just came out sounding tired. He didn't try to get the glass back.

Max sighed. "Whether you decide to call a shrink or not, brother, this phase is over. We're calling it."

"What are you talking about?"

The chef exchanged a nod with the bartender, who

shot Sean a guilty glance. "Sorry, Sean. Big Mitch called a few minutes ago. You're cut off."

"What?" This was the last thing he'd expected. Nagging him to get help he could deal with. Bringing Big Mitch into the picture was a little extreme. The head of River Hill's resident biker gang was a silent owner of The Hut, a fact not many people knew. Except the other small business owners of River Hill, of course. "What the hell did you do?" he said, turning on Max.

Iain laid a hand on Sean's back, warm through the fabric of his vintage tee. "Sorry, lad. It's done. I'm afraid you won't be served at any bar in town."

"You …" Sean seethed. He couldn't even get words out.

"It's for your own good," Max said. "You'll thank us later. Maybe."

"I don't give a shit whether you thank us or not," Noah added. "I just want you upright and alive by the end of the year, and this is the only way we could see to make that happen."

"I'll just go out of town to drink, then." Sean rolled his eyes. "Your perfect plan has some pretty big holes in it, guys."

"Well, that's your choice," Noah said. "But I have to tell you this particular plan was Plan B."

"What was Plan A?" Did he even want to know?

Noah sighed. "Angelica just got a seat on the tourism board. With your mom." Noah's girlfriend was a former actress who'd opened a bed and breakfast in River Hill last year, leveraging her former career to get a deal with a TV network to film the renovation. The show had brought a lot of good publicity to River Hill, and pretty much everybody adored her these days. Including Sean's mother, who owned the family bakery. Where he now worked.

The only thing he did these days besides drink, and the only thing that had given him a lifeline when it had felt like his entire world had spun out of control, was head to the bakery. He'd come home to River Hill to work, hoping the familiar actions of kneading, cutting, and baking would soothe his bruised soul after what had happened in L.A.

But his mother didn't know about the drinking part, as far as he knew.

"I hate your girlfriend," he told Noah. "And you can tell her I said so."

"You can tell her yourself if you do it sober," Noah said. "And she told me to tell *you* that."

Sean shook the bleariness of sobriety out of his eyes as he bent over a sheet of scone dough. His head was aching more than it usually did on the days he was hungover.

He sliced mechanically through the thick dough on a diagonal with his bench scraper, the movement economical as only years of practice could make it. He might have spent the last ten years in L.A. working his way up the ladder as a record producer, but he'd grown up doing this. Baking was in his bones. The Amory family had owned The Breadery since River Hill had been founded.

He slid the scones onto a waiting sheet pan and popped them into the huge oven, pulling out two oversized muffin tins before he closed the door. He prodded the muffins with a finger, then spun the tins onto the counter to cool enough that he could turn out the goodies inside and put them into the display case before opening. Which he wasn't looking forward to.

It was the quiet mornings alone in the bakery that had brought him back here. Sometimes, he thought the bakery had saved his life. He'd been shell-shocked, shattered after finding his protégé dead. Producing records had suddenly seemed like an incredible waste of time. A week after he'd buried the kid, Sean had returned to the one thing he knew he could do productively: feeding people. When he'd asked for the opening shift, the bakery's other employees had practically thrown him a party. His mother hadn't asked any questions either. She'd simply handed over the keys and a couple of quick instructions he hadn't really needed.

It turned out baking was like riding a bike. You never really forgot how, especially when every turn of the dough, every shake of the sifter, and every sprinkle of cinnamon brought color back into your pale, dry life.

But he still hadn't been able to shake the nightmares. So he'd been drinking. Maybe his friends were right, though, and it was too much.

Today was the first morning in ages he hadn't merely gone through the motions of mixing, scooping, rolling, and flipping. The line of pastries already in the display case shone softly in the light, sugar crystals winking slightly. Sean sighed and rested his head against the side of the huge refrigerator.

Sobriety might be healthy, but it was hard as shit. He wanted a drink.

Instead, he swept the used parchment paper and crumbs lining the countertop into a trash bag and spun it swiftly to bring the ends together. He tied a knot in the top and hooked a finger through it, lifting the bag and taking it to the back door toward the dumpster, which was cleverly disguised behind a faux picket fence. Because this was River Hill, and everything was relentlessly pretty here. Even the dumpsters.

Sean heaved the bag over the edge of the fence, then paused to admire the sunrise for a brief moment before going back inside to start on his next batch of danishes. Picket fences, window boxes full to bursting with color, and delicate filigree gazebos were one thing; this was real beauty.

The Breadery opened at seven in the morning for folks who wanted a quick breakfast pastry to go with their coffee from The Hollow Bean across the town square. That meant he arrived no later than four to prepare the morning's offerings. A few doughs got made by whoever closed the night before—usually his mom and one of the other employees—but the quick breads and all the decorative work had to get done before the sun came up.

He stretched, feeling his back crack, then paused as he heard an unexpected sound. Was that somebody running? His body came alert without conscious thought, years of living in L.A. taking his mind into danger mode immediately. He wasn't about to deal with another tragedy, especially not here on his home turf. Just the thought of seeing another dead body here, in his safe haven, made his blood boil. He turned, ready to do something—although he wasn't entirely sure what—and saw the source of the running footsteps.

It was only a jogger. His body sagged, then straightened as he got a closer look. She was toned and lean, but with just enough curves in all the right places. Tanned skin wrapped in black compression leggings and a purple tank that left the lines of her shoulders bare to the thin morning light. Long dark hair, swept back into a thick ponytail, swung with every rhythmic step. She slowed as she came closer to the bakery, and he stepped back, not wanting to get in her way. His back hit the doorframe, and he watched, enraptured, as she slowed to a walk. The woman took deep breaths, lifting her head and closing her eyes. It seemed like she was sniffing the air. Then again, perhaps she was. He was mostly used to it, but the heady scents coming from the ovens were most potent at this time of day.

His foot scuffed the ground, and her eyes flew open. When she saw him staring, he felt himself blushing like a teenager. It was like she'd caught him peeping. He raised a hand awkwardly, and she smiled at him, then sped past without a word. A few long steps later, she was gone, jogging around the corner and into the foot traffic of a River Hill morning.

Sean let out a breath he hadn't noticed he was holding. Well, *that* was something new. If he saw beauty like that every time he took a break in the morning, he'd come out to admire the sunrise a hell of a lot more often.

As it was, this was the first morning he'd taken even a moment out of the simple routine he'd clung to as a lifeline when he came home. And to be honest, it was the first morning in months he'd been sober enough to appreciate anything anyhow. Had she been there all along?

What else had he been missing?

⁂

Chapter Two

*J*essica Casillas-Moore sagged through her front door. Bent over at the waist, she took a few deep breaths before straightening. She raised her arm and tapped the screen on her digital watch to gauge her progress. Three miles. Not bad. Not great either, but some days getting out of bed for a pre-dawn run was harder than others. If she were being honest with herself, that was the case more often than not these days.

Fanning the long, chocolate brown hair off the back of her neck as she made her way to the bathroom at the back of her tiny cottage, Jess wondered if it was time to reconsider her priorities in life. She'd won a few pageants when she was younger, and she'd managed to leverage her so-called 'beauty queen' status into both a successful beauty blog and, most recently, a job as a lifestyle 'guru' for a few local TV stations. But she couldn't remember the last time she'd enjoyed a meal with friends or family without counting the calories of everything she consumed. She had friends who swore by skinny margaritas and oven-baked tortilla chips, but as far as Jess was concerned, she'd rather have the real thing or nothing at all.

Which brought to mind the route she'd traversed this morning. After attending her niece's birthday party a handful of weeks ago and not eating any of the prettily-decorated cupcakes or cookies from The Breadery, River Hill's famous bakery, she'd taken to running past there every morning instead. If she couldn't *eat* any of their baked goods, Jess reasoned inhaling the sweet, buttery scent was close to the next best thing. Although after the handsome—if slightly bleary-eyed—baker had caught her sniffing the air this morning, she might have to reconsider that plan.

Now, Jess peeled the sweaty athletic gear from her body and stood naked in front of the mirror on her closet door, turning this way and that to inspect her reflection. Even with constant diet and exercise, some of her natural curves were a bit softer than they'd once been, and her breasts didn't sit quite so high up as they had even a year ago. She cupped them and then dropped her hands away, watching the weighty flesh bounce and then settle back into place.

She'd always heard a woman's body changed drastically once she hit thirty, and with that date looming in the not-too-distant future, Jess wondered what other changes she could expect. She turned and stared back over her shoulder at her rear, surveying it for any new signs of cellulite. Between the fifteen miles she ran each week and the squats and lunges her trainer made her do three times a week, it was arguably her best feature. Even so, as someone whose professional longevity was tied to her beauty, she knew all too well that age and gravity waited for no woman.

With a weary sigh, she turned on the hot water and waited for the bathroom to steam up. Grabbing a new razor from a basket under the sink, she stepped into the shower while giving herself a pep talk. It was no use getting depressed before brunch with her family. Her two older brothers—with their constant nagging about when she was finally going to settle down and start having babies—could be counted on to darken her mood all by themselves.

"*E*at up, mija." Celia Casillas, Jessica's abuela, patted her shoulder as she made her way to the stove. "You're too skinny. Men like a woman with meat on her bones."

"If I eat any of this," Jess said, gesturing to the chips, salsa, and guacamole spread out on the kitchen table in front of her, "I won't have room for your albondigas or papa's tri-tip."

"And we know how much Jess likes her balls," her sister Marisol cackled as she grabbed three Coronas from the refrigerator on her way through the kitchen to join their brothers Robert and Manny in the backyard.

"Not as much as you love *your* meat," Jess replied through a pasted-on grin as the screen door clanged shut. She loved her siblings, but as the youngest of four, she'd been the butt of their jokes her whole damn life. As a kid, she'd assumed they'd all grow out of it, but she hadn't been that lucky.

Jess's grandmother set a beer down in front of her. "Ignore her. She's just trying to get under your skin."

"Well, she's doing a pretty good job of it. She knows it's inappropriate to talk like that in front of you. Heck, in front of anyone."

"You know your sister. She likes to shock people." Her grandma settled into the chair across from Jess and loaded a tortilla chip up with homemade salsa. She brought it to her mouth but halted just before taking a bite. "She's jealous, you know?"

Jess snorted and shook her head. "No way. She thinks I'm pathetic." That was one of the things that hurt the most about her relationship with her siblings. Jess had worked hard for years to get where she was—first with beauty pageants, and then with building her own consulting business, and now her YouTube channel, blog, and stints as a lifestyle expert on local news and radio shows.

She'd worked full time while putting herself through school, and while she might not have a life that mirrored the rest of her family's, she'd built something to be proud of. She had made a name for herself, but lately, it seemed like the only time anyone cared was when she could get them free stuff. Otherwise, all they ever did was tease her about her diet, her makeup, or the lack of a man in her life.

The first two she could handle. Jess knew she'd chosen a career path that some might consider shallow, but the constant jibes about her thinking she was too good for any of the men they introduced her to were low blows. She wasn't arrogant or stuck-up; she was *discerning*. Why that was a bad thing, she didn't know. With the divorce rate so high in her extended family, she would have thought they'd applaud her for not settling for less than she deserved. Instead, her brothers and sister used her single status to mock her. It wasn't like she *liked* going home to an empty house each night.

Chewing around her food, her grandma said, "No, mija. She spends her days carting the boys to and from school and then going to PTA meetings and practices, and now she wishes she'd made different choices when she was younger. I love Marisol—and I would kill for my grandbabies—but she should have waited to have those kids. She wasn't ready, and neither was that no-good Jason."

Jess had always considered Marisol—five years her senior—the beauty of their family. In fact, she was the reason Jess had gotten involved in pageants to begin with —she'd wanted to be just like her big sister when she grew up. Back then Marisol had had it all … or so Jess had thought. But when she was twenty, she'd gotten knocked up by Jason, her on-again-off-again boyfriend. Their "off again" periods usually followed her catching him cheating, but for some inexplicable reason, Marisol always took him back. When she'd become pregnant with Jason Junior, she'd dropped out of college, and she and Jay got married. Two years later and pregnant with their second kid, she found out he'd been cheating on her *again*. The ink wasn't even dry on their divorce papers when their second son was born. Marisol was a good mother, but it hadn't always been easy on her. Jess knew that. They *all* knew it. That's why she, Robert, and Manny took the opportunity to help out whenever they could. That was just how their family worked. They'd grown up with a single mother themselves, and they all knew how hard it was. But while Marisol had grown closer to their brothers as her sons had grown up, she and Jess had somehow drifted further apart.

Never once in all these years had Jess considered her sister could be envious of her; she'd just assumed she'd done something to anger Marisol but couldn't figure out what it might have been. Now, hearing her abuela's theory, Jess wondered if the older woman wasn't on to something.

"I don't know, maybe." She shrugged and nibbled on a chip. She loved her grandma's guacamole, but the fats from the avocado did better things for her hair than they did for her thighs. She'd be better off going home and applying it as a conditioning mask than she would by filling her belly with it.

"There's no maybe about it," her grandmother declared as she headed back to the stove. "Now go tell your sister and those boys to help your papa bring in the meat, and we can finally eat. I'm starving."

Jess rose and planted a kiss on her grandmother's cheek. "You're the best."

The other woman pretended to wave away the praise but then smiled. "I really am."

*J*ess stepped outside, the warm evening breeze a welcome respite from the fragrance of her grandmother's cooking. A woman on a life-long diet could only be surrounded by the delicious smell of onions, garlic, and tomatoes for so long without pushing everyone to the side and shoving her head inside the pot.

At least out here, she could stand down-wind from the grill. And honestly, except for her grandmother's meatballs, Jess wasn't really a beef girl anyway. Just another way she differed from everyone else in her family. While her brothers could put away literal pounds of carne asada and her sister had never met a tri-tip she didn't like, Jess stuck to the grilled zucchini her papa always made especially for her instead.

"Hey, you guys," Jess said as she came up alongside her siblings. "Soup's almost ready, so Abuela wants everyone to head inside."

Manny finished typing something on his phone, and then shoved the device into his back pocket. "That was Rosalie. She needs me to pick up Abigail."

"I thought it was her weekend," Marisol sneered, hefting one of the platters and turning toward the house. There was no love lost between Marisol and Rosie, whose younger sister was one of the girls Jason had cheated on Marisol with. Marisol couldn't believe her brother would betray her by literally sleeping with the enemy, while *he* failed to understand how Rosalie was responsible for her sister's behavior. It was an argument Jess could practically recite by heart.

"It is, but something came up."

Robert rolled his eyes. "That seems to happen a lot lately." He wasn't a fan of Rosalie either, but that stemmed more from the fact that when she had come into the picture, Manny hadn't been able to act as his wingman anymore. At thirty-five, Robert Casillas-Moore was the biggest ladies' man Jess knew.

"It is what it is." Manny sighed and grabbed the other platter, while Jess picked up the small plate of vegetables and raced to catch up with her siblings.

"It doesn't have to be," Robert said, as Jess fell into step next to them.

"He's right. You should talk with your lawyer again about the custody arrangement." She knew her advice wasn't wanted, but she couldn't help it.

Manny shot her an angry look as Robert jogged ahead to hold the door open for them. "And do what—ask for full-time custody? You know I can't do that."

"Why?" Jess honestly didn't get it. Manny was a talented animator who worked from home, so he had plenty of time for his daughter. And his house, while small like Jess's, was a much better environment than his ex-wife's place in what real estate agents liked to call a "transitional neighborhood." The real issue, she suspected, was that Manny's new girlfriend Camila didn't want his young daughter around. Camila was smart and beautiful, but she also had a jealous streak a mile wide and a foot deep. The fact that Jess's brother had been married before did *not* sit well with her.

Frankly, Jess didn't see their relationship working out in the long run, but what did she know about things like that? She hadn't been on a real date in six months and hadn't had a boyfriend in way longer than that.

Which her brother, of course, was always quick to point out. He pushed his way through the door with a huff. "Honestly, Jess. You are so naive sometimes."

"Manuel Joseph Casillas Moore! You be nice to your sister." With a look that brooked no argument, their grandma set a big, steaming bowl of soup in the middle of the table.

Manny's jaw ticked, and Jess knew he was biting back a smart-ass reply. He shook his head and joined Marisol on the opposite side of the room. Setting his platter down next to hers on the antique oak sideboard, he turned and crossed his arms over his chest. "Someday you're going to have to grow up and join the rest of us adults in the real world. Maybe then you'll understand."

Marisol snorted and rolled her eyes. "Not likely. Jess is waiting for Prince Charming to come along and sweep her off her feet. Everything will be perfectly sickening, and they'll spend all their time riding around on unicorns and living in their made-up fairytale world."

Jess felt tears springing into her eyes. Her sister's idea of humor felt a lot more like an attack. She breathed deeply and stared hard at her siblings, wondering when they'd become so bitter. Wondering what she'd ever done to deserve this treatment. All three stared back, the look on each of their faces defiant and stubborn.

She looked away first. She didn't have the energy for this today. "I'm sorry, abuela, but I'm not hungry anymore. If you'll excuse me—" She darted across the room and grabbed her purse, rushing out the front door before anybody could stop her. She cried for the entire fifteen-minute journey back to her house.

When she pulled into the driveway, her stomach rumbled loudly. Of course.

Jess slammed her palm against the steering wheel. She let out a frustrated growl and pushed herself out of the car. Stalking angrily up the walk, she unlocked her front door and stepped over the threshold, tossing her purse on the table to her right. At least now she wouldn't have to work off her grandmother's meal by adding an extra mile to tomorrow's run.

Unbidden, her thoughts flashed to the man standing outside The Breadery. The one with dark, haunted eyes and overgrown scruff. The one who'd set her heart racing even more than it already had been. The one who'd stared at her and who she'd stared right back at. Briefly, Jess wondered what had made his eyes so sad, and if he'd seen her own sadness reflected back at him.

Hmm. Maybe she'd keep that extra mile after all.

ACKNOWLEDGMENTS

From Rebecca

As always, a million and one thanks to my husband who who is a saint among men. I couldn't do this without his support.

A huge thanks also goes out to our beta readers who continue to provide valuable insight and suggestions that help make our characters that much better.

And of course, I can't forget the book bloggers who've supported me along the way and have been enthusiastic about the River Hill Series since I first teased you with the words "sexy winemaker." I hope you love this dashing distiller too!

And finally, to Jamaila … my soul sister. I am so, so glad we decided to write together. This has been such an amazing experience, and I hope we're still doing it when we're both old and gray. (PS, tell the husband I'm sorry about all the texts.)

From Jamaila

Thanks always and foremost to my husband, who is still putting up with this bizarre career choice of mine. And special thanks to my children, who are both the reason I write and the reason I never have time to write.

A huge thank you to my BFF and beta reader Robin, who is always super enthusiastic about these books (and always willing to have playdates, especially with mimosas).

I have never-ending wells of gratitude for the book bloggers, bookstagrammers, tweeters, and reviewers who have embraced River Hill—if I could, I'd invite you all to a huge party in that adorable town square and dinner at Frankie's afterwards.

And finally, most importantly, thank you to Rebecca, my partner in crime and wine. For a hundred texts, instant messages, and emails, and for messages of increasing enthusiasm as the time difference gets greater. I can't wait for our next retreat, and I can't wait to keep writing with you no matter where we are!

ABOUT THE AUTHORS

Rebecca Norinne and Jamaila Brinkley have been friends for almost fifteen years. Separately, they write contemporary romance and historical fantasy romance; together, they created the enchanting world of River Hill. In this charming Northern California town, Norinne and Brinkley combined the interests that made them friends in the first place—great food, delicious wine, and a pinch of home renovation—and added in the spicy romance they love.

Rebecca lives in Massachusetts with her husband, and Jamaila lives in Maryland with her husband and twin children. They email each other a lot.

Rebecca: http://www.rebeccanorinne.com
Jamaila: https://jamailabrinkley.wordpress.com

Steamy Standalones
Hollywood Dreams
Secrets and Lies

ALSO BY JAMAILA BRINKLEY

THE WIZARDS OF LONDON SERIES
Thieves' Honor
Witch's Stone
Captain's Lady

THE GALIPP FILES
The Star of Anatolia
The Mathematical Gambit
The Portrait Problem